For Milie and Will,
obviously

Pirate McSnottbeard

IN THE
ZOMBIE TERROR RAMPAGE

Pirate

McSnottbeard

IN THE
ZOMBIE TERROR RAMPAGE

PAUL WHITFIELD

WALKER
BOOKS

First published in Great Britain 2017 by Walker Books Ltd
87 Vauxhall Walk, London SE11 5HJ

2 4 6 8 10 9 7 5 3 1

This book has been typeset in Stempel Schneidler and LTC Pabst Oldstyle

Printed and bound in Great Britain by Clays Ltd, St Ives plc

British Library Cataloguing in Publication Data:
a catalogue record for this book is
available from the British Library

ISBN 978-1-4063-7308-0

www.walker.co.uk

NOBODY DIES

Nobody dies in this book.

I think you should know that right from the start. This story is scary enough without thinking that someone might meet a nasty end – or an end of any sort. So don't worry about anyone dying, because they don't. The second thing you should know, though I already mentioned it, is that this book is scary.

Really, really,

SUPER SCARY.

How scary?

Dinosaur-scary, volcano-scary, zombie-scary, warlock-scary, house-devouring-whirlpool-scary, flesh-eating-bugs-scary and werewolves-scary.

And even scarier than that, because this book also has the super-huge-most-scary-thing in the whole world: **PIRATES!**

The **PIRATES** in this book are so scary that you have to write

LIKE THIS, IN BIG CAPITALS

whenever you mention them.

Also in this book is my brother William, age eleven. That's him just there.

I call him Will, and you can too.

He's the hero.

You'll see why soon enough.

Every book needs a hero – especially super-scary books. Without a hero the scary things would just stick around even after you've said "THE END", and no one wants that. That's why I'm lucky to have Will.

Sure, he's grumpy almost all of the time. And he never wants to play dressing-up or catch insects with me. And, yes, he makes me look bad by eating all his beans when I've eaten barely any of my beans. Everyone knows that beans are gross, even if they help you grow up strong.

That's what my dad always says: "Eat your beans or you won't grow up strong." I always say: "I don't even want to be strong, I want to be smart." So he says: "Well it isn't very smart to not eat your beans." If I was smart I'd know how to respond to that – then I wouldn't have to eat beans.

Anyway, even with the grumpiness and beans-eating, I'm still lucky Will is around.

Oh, I should probably introduce myself too. I'm Emilie, age nine. I like climbing things, but I'm afraid of heights; I'm disorganized, but love making lists; I'm good at school, but always get in trouble for doodling; and I'm prone to screaming in fright, but … no, actually, there is

no "but" on that one. I just really do scream a lot
when I get scared. And, if I'm being honest, I get
scared kind of easily. Which is another reason
why I'm lucky to have Will for a brother.

I was lucky to have him for a brother *before*
the worst, most horrible, really-scariest-thing-ever
happened. But I was *especially* lucky to have him
for a brother the day our house got washed out
to sea and our parents were kidnapped by
PIRATES!

PIRATES!

Here are five things you should know about
PIRATES:

Things Worth Knowing No. 1
by Emilie

1) You almost always smell PIRATES
before you hear them.
They hate washing,
never wipe their bums
and smell like rotting fish.

2) You almost always hear PIRATES before you see them. PIRATES are always shouting.

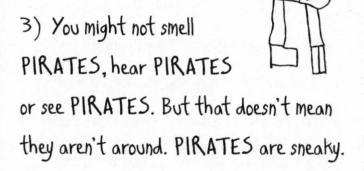

3) You might not smell PIRATES, hear PIRATES or see PIRATES. But that doesn't mean they aren't around. PIRATES are sneaky.

4) PIRATES are nasty too. Whatever they do, they do it in the worst way you can imagine, and normally worse than that.

5) If you see PIRATES, run!
Run as fast as you can. Don't
stop until you can't see them.
Then, when you catch your breath
again, run until you can't hear them.
Then run some more. Run until your
sides hurt and your knees ache and the
last whiff of them has evaporated and
you think you are safe. Then run! Run
faster and further than you did before,
because when you think you are safe the

 PIRATES are probably
about to grab you.

A WHIFF OF DANGER

The morning that the worst, most horrible, really-scariest-thing-ever happened, I woke, stretched, scratched my belly and knew straight away something was wrong.

People always say that: "I knew something was wrong." What they usually mean is they discovered something was wrong way after it was already obvious to everyone. Then, because they look silly, they say, "I knew something was wrong." So here is some advice: if you really know, or even just think, something is wrong, say so straight away. Which is what I did. And that's how you know that I really knew something was wrong.

I went straight into Will's room.

"Will. Something is wrong!" I said.

"Go away," Will grumbled and pulled his pillow over his head.

"The house smells like fish," I said.

Will lifted the pillow off his head and looked at me.

"Emilie," he said slowly, in the serious voice he uses when I put a dress on the toy monkey he pretends not to sleep with. "Take a look outside."

I went over to the window and opened the curtains.

"William!" I said, a bit louder. "Something is very, very wrong! The house smells like rotten fish, Dad's old trainers and the cat's toilet."

"**PIRATES!**" said Will.

"YEAH," I shouted, though I wasn't listening to him. "But I don't really care about the smell any more, because the house, this house, *our* house, is floating in the ocean!"

Just then a fish jumped out of the water and smacked into the window.

"ARGHHH!" I screamed. "Did you say

PIRATES?!"

"We need Mum and Dad," said Will, still using his monkey-dressed-in-a-frock voice, as he came over to the window.

"ARGHHH!" I screamed again, but this time because Will had grabbed me and was dragging me down the hall to Mum and Dad's room.

"MUM! DAD!" shouted Will.

"HELP!" I shouted – which is an improvement

on ARGHHH!, though I might still have been shouting ARGHHH! too.

Anyway, I bet you can't guess what we found when we got to their room.

Did you guess? What did you guess?

Did you guess a baby giraffe wearing a dress and a Viking's helmet, riding a tricycle?

WRONG!

WHAT WE FOUND

What we found was nothing.

Well, not exactly nothing. We found a huge mess. The window was open and water was slopping into the room. There was a prawn flipping about on Mum's pillow and I think I saw an octopus peep out of Dad's sock drawer.

What we didn't find was Mum or Dad.

"The **PIRATES** have got them," said Will.

"What do you mean, *got them*?" I asked. "Got them what? Got them a present? Got them breakfast? Got them a—"

"Shush," said Will, walking over to the window. "Listen."

Here is a list of the five things I hate most in the world:

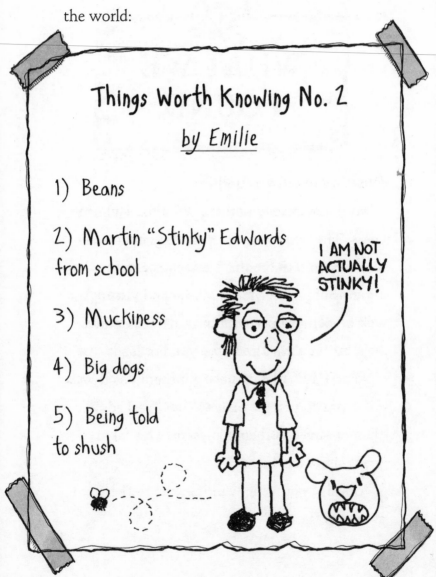

That's not necessarily in order. If I'm eating beans, then beans will be top of the list. If Martin "Stinky" Edwards is pulling my hair, then Martin "Stinky" Edwards will be at the top. And if someone is telling me to shush – well, you get the idea.

So if there's one way to make sure I don't shush, it's to tell me to shush.

And right at that moment, there was no way I was going to shush. What I was going to do was scream. But the thing about screaming is, if you want to do it really well, and by really well I mean *really loud*, then you have to take a big breath first. And when you're taking that big breath, whether you want to or not, you end up shushing for a bit. And in that bit of shush before I screamed I heard … singing.

PIRATES CAN'T SING

Actually, it wasn't exactly singing, it was more just shouting that rhymed, which is apparently what passes for singing among **PIRATES**. Either way, it was so awful I completely forgot to scream.

This is what I heard:

"Hoist up dear old Mummy,
Tie her to the mast.
Rope Daddy to the wheel,
And spin him super fast.

Tickle their feet with feathers,
Put chillies up their nose.
Paint their knees with honey,
            And feed 'em to the crows.

Put them in a little cage,
Take them to the zoo.
Charge a buck a gander,
That's what we're gonna do."

I looked at Will. "Mum hates chillies," I said.

"Even more when they are up her nose in a zoo," he agreed.

OUT THE WINDOW

Here's another thing you should know about **PIRATES**: they are always singing.

It's the thing they love doing most in the world – after shouting, fighting, kidnapping, bullying, robbing, hijacking, arguing, eating with their fingers, throwing food, burping, picking their noses, farting on each other, pulling cats' tails, breaking toys, making babies cry, drawing on school desks, cleaning out their ears with kitchen spoons, stealing and making a mess then refusing to tidy up.

But for now, let's concentrate on the singing.

The amazing thing about the **PIRATES'** singing, apart from its amazing awfulness, was

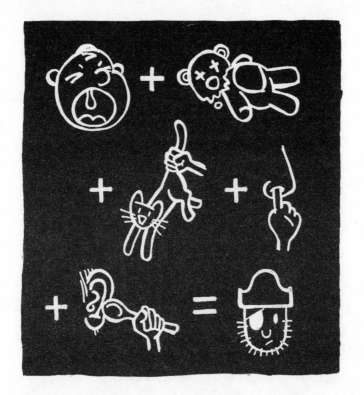

that it was coming from just outside the house.

The **PIRATES** were close.

We ran over to my parents' window and looked out – to be honest, I was interested to see how angry Dad would be with whoever was spinning him on a wheel.

This is what we saw:

"WOW," I said.

"WOW,"

said Will.

ZOOS

We stared out the window at the **PIRATE** ship.

You are probably thinking we should have sprung into action to rescue our parents. But it's not every day you see a huge **PIRATE** ship floating just outside your house, so it's worth stopping to look at it.

And there was one other thing. You see, we had to catch the **PIRATES**, but we were floating in a house and they were in a boat. On land, a house is just as fast as a boat. But when it comes to water, a boat has significant advantages – such as being a boat. The **PIRATES** may have been close, but they were still too far away for us to do anything other than watch them. So we watched.

"Do you think they were serious about putting Mum and Dad in a zoo?" I asked Will. "It's just that, in a zoo they'd be looked after. And we could visit them whenever we wanted."

I was also thinking that if they were in a zoo they wouldn't be around to tell us to go to bed or turn the iPad off.

"A zoo doesn't sound too bad," I said.

"Depends which part of the zoo they put them in," said Will. "Have you ever smelt a hippopotamus up close? Anyway, that bit about the crows eating their knees didn't sound too good."

MUM AND DAD
(Parentus Domesticus)

THE MAP

"If we're going to save Mum and Dad we're going to need the map," said Will.

"The what?" I asked.

"The map. **PIRATES** always leave a map." Will walked across the bedroom and tore the duvet off Mum and Dad's bed. "When we find it it'll show us where they're going and probably where we can find their treasure. Leaving a map is kind of a thing with **PIRATES**."

Will began pulling socks and underpants out of drawers, flinging pillows aside, turning over bedside tables, dragging Mum's best dresses from the cupboard and tossing Dad's business suits on the floor.

He was having so much fun messing up the

room I almost didn't want to interrupt him.

"Do you think *that* might be it?" I asked, pointing at a scroll pinned to the wall with a dagger.

WHAT MY BROTHER DOES ON MONDAYS

This is what was on the paper: 👉

YE AULD TREASURE MAP!

PROPERTY OF
DASHING McSNOTTBEARD
NUMBARRR 1, DANGERWAY,
TREASUREVILLE, PIRATE ISLE

"That doesn't look much help," I said.

"Try turning it over," said Will.

"That's not much help either," I said.

I was wrong.

The first thing the map told us was that the PIRATE *McSnottbeard* had kidnapped our parents.

This, apparently, was bad news.

"He's the most horrible, most cruel and most stupid PIRATE in the whole world," said Will. "Of the 138 PIRATES known to sail the high seas, he is ranked No. 1 for SMELLINESS, No. 1 for DESPICABILITY and No. 2 for HAIRINESS. He's just two whiskers behind *Hairy-Harry Beardypants*."

"Despica-what?" I asked.

"Horribleness," said Will.

"Oh," I said, though I had no idea what he was talking about.

"On the plus side he is also ranked No. 1 for STUPIDITY and No. 2 for MAKING GENERALLY BAD DECISIONS, behind *Wrong-Way McGubbins*."

"Will," I said. "How do you know so much about **PIRATES?**"

"Oh, that," Will mumbled. "Well the thing is, I kind of, that is to say, ummm… You know how each Monday I have football practice after school?"

"Yeah."

"Well, it's kind of not true," said Will, looking down at his feet.

"What kind of not true?"

"The kind of not true that some people might call lying," said Will.

"What *do* you do?" I asked.

"I hunt **PIRATES**," said Will. "I am a **PIRATE** hunter. At least, on Monday nights I am."

I was a bit miffed about the lying. But I was relieved too. Having a **PIRATE** hunter in the family was going to be handy.

"Are you any good?" I asked.

"I am the best," Will said, looking up and fixing me with a stare that made me shiver.

"Stop looking at me like that, you weirdo," I said as I folded the map and slipped it in my pocket. "What else do you know about *McSnottbeard*?"

WANTED
FOR PIRACY & NASTINESS

McSNOTTBEARD
REWARD
10 DOUBLOONS

McSNOTTBEARD

"He is definitely the most horrible, most cruel and most stupid **PIRATE** in the whole world," said Will.

"You already said that."

"He is so horrible," Will went on, "that he once stole all the false teeth from all the grandads in France, just for fun. He is so cruel that he left each toothless grandad a crunchy red apple, just because they couldn't eat them.

"And he is so stupid that he accidentally left one of those little fruit stickers with his name and address on each apple. The police went straight to his hideout and found all the teeth."

barrr 1,
rway,
reville,
E Island.

"His name and address!" I shouted.

I turned the map over again and there it was:

Numbarrr 1,

Dangerway,

Treasureville,

PIRATE Isle.

"So we know where they're going," I said.

"Yep," said Will, wandering back over to the window.

"So all we have to do is wait for a boat to come by, get a lift to **PIRATE** Isle and get Mum and Dad back."

"Good plan," said Will, shaking his head.

"Why are you shaking your head?"

"It's just…"

"What?"

"It's probably nothing."

"Tell me."

"There was that other thing on the map that has me a bit worried."

I looked back at the map.

THAT OTHER THING

The thing is, all this time while I had been running around screaming, and octopuses were hiding in Dad's sock drawer, and the **PIRATES** were singing and Will was explaining why he's rubbish at football (I'd always wondered why he was so bad), the house was bobbing along through the water.

Look again at that map. Go on.

Put your finger on the X next to the arrow that says "You" (which was actually me and Will). Now trace it along the dotted line that goes out beneath the skull and crossbones and go around

the first corner a bit. You see where the line crosses over itself? That was where the house was by this time.

We were still bobbing along and keeping up with the **PIRATE** boat. Only we weren't really just bobbing along any more. We were kind of surging through the water – or we would've been if the water hadn't been surging just as fast as us.

Now put your finger back on the map. Put it in that same spot as before and then follow the line along a little bit more until you get to that big black scribble thing. What does it say just there?

"A GREAT BIG WHIRLPOOL!" said Will, who was looking out the window, but probably repeating exactly the same thing you just said.

A GREAT BIG WHIRLPOOL!

This is what Riskypedia says about whirlpools:

RISKYPEDIA
The Adventurer's Encyclopedia

>> WHIRLPOOL
Whirlpool Corporation is an American business well-known for making washing machines and fridges, but this probably isn't what you are looking for.

Hang on.

Wrong one.

Here it is:

RISKYPEDIA
The Adventurer's Encyclopedia

>> WHIRLPOOL

A whirlpool is a rotating mass of
water formed by conflicting currents.
Most whirlpools are harmless. Powerful
whirlpools, which are called maelstroms,
are not harmless. In fact, they are
massively destructive and usually lethal.
Maelstroms are best avoided.

A GREAT BIG MAELSTROM!

"The whirlpool is sucking us in," said Will.

"I think you'll find it is actually a *maelstrom*," I said, feeling rather smart. I was preparing to explain the differences between whirlpools and maelstroms when the house suddenly tipped sideways. So what I actually said was "ARGHHH!" I warned you earlier that I'm prone to screaming.

"Quick," said Will, "we've got to get out."

I didn't move. I stared out the window at the rushing water sucking us towards a roaring black hole.

SNOTTY EMOTION

The house was moving fast, dipping lower in the ocean as we gained speed. Inky water flooded through the window, freezing me up to the knees. I reached out a hand to hold on to the windowsill.

Across the spinning water I could see the ship. The **PIRATES** had stopped singing. They were panicking and shouting now, which was a lot like their singing, only perhaps more tuneful.

Will came up beside me.

"Emilie, we *have* to get out of here," he said gently. "If we stay, we'll drown."

"If we go outside we'll drown too," I said.

"Probably," said Will. "But probably is the best odds we're going to get."

He had a point.

We climbed the stairs to the top floor and then through the attic window onto the roof. From there we made our way to the chimney, held on and looked out at the maelstrom.

Will took my hand. "Emilie," he said, "if we don't get out of this alive – you've been a really good sister."

That might not sound like much, but it was just about the nicest thing Will had ever said to me. I began to cry. I wanted to say something nice to him, but each time I opened my mouth I sobbed.

I ended up just blowing my nose on my nightie. I think he knew what I meant.

MUM AND DAD

As the house slid further into the maelstrom, the **PIRATE** ship edged closer to us. I got a good look at *McSnottbeard* and his crew for the first time.

They were as horrible to see as they were to hear.

There were five of them including *McSnottbeard*, who was easy to pick out due to his general hairiness and his **PIRATE** hat.

"What have you done with our parents?" Will shouted across the waves.

McSnottbeard let out a wicked laugh as he looked up to the ship's sails.

"Arrr, they're hanging around somewhere," he chuckled.

I followed his gaze.

"EMILIE! WILLIAM!" my parents shouted.

The house bounced over a wave and sank deeper into the water. I held tighter to the chimney.

"We're coming to save you!" I yelled, though I wasn't sure that's what was happening.

"Good!" shouted Dad.

"Only, where's your jacket?"

BETTY BLUNDER

GRUNT

DASHING McSNOTTBEARD

"What?" I yelled.

"You'll catch a cold."

I looked down at our sinking house, then over at Will. "Is he serious?"

"Parents." Will shrugged. "They can't help themselves."

Our house tilted further into the maelstrom, leaning us closer to the **PIRATE** ship.

PISTOL
PETE

DOTTY
DAGGER

DEAD
DAN

REMEMBERED
HERE·FOR·HE
WILL NOT
BE IN THIS
STORY

"Give us back our parents!" I shouted at *McSnottbeard*.

"Go smoke a kipper," he called back.

I turned to Will. "What did he say?"

"I think he told you to go smoke a kipper."

"A kipper?"

"Yeah."

"Is that rude?"

"Rather."

For those of you still scratching your head about kippers, this is what Riskypedia says:

RISKYPEDIA
The Adventurer's Encyclopedia

>> KIPPER
A kipper is a herring, which is itself a fish, cut down the middle and then flavoured with smoke from a fire. Typically eaten for breakfast in Britain, they smell awful but taste delicious.

I hate rude people – I should have put that in my list of things I hate.

Just at that moment I hated them even more than beans. And *McSnottbeard* was about the rudest person I'd ever met.

I started to get mad. The madness grew and grew until it was so big it pushed out most of the scared.

"Will," I said, "we are *not* going to drown."

I think I may have been doing that same squinty-eyed stare that Will was doing a few pages back.

"We are going to get Mum and Dad back. And we are going to get *McSnottbeard*. And when we do we are going to make HIM smoke a kipper!"

"That's right," said Will.

THEN EVERYTHING WENT BLACK.

REALLY

BLACK.

CENTRE FUNGAL MAGIC

In the darkness the house tipped sideways and started to spin.

I slid down the roof. The water, which was even blacker than the rest of the blackness, edged closer. My feet slipped over the gutter of the roof and— I stopped.

It was the strangest thing. The house was on its side. The roof was where the wall should have been, the wall was where the roof should have been, and I was where no child should ever be. And I was stuck fast.

"Will," I shouted. "Are you there?"

"Right next to you," came the reply from
right next to me.

"Why aren't we falling?"

"Centrifugal force," said Will.

"Centre fungal what?"

"Centrifugal," he said – as if repeating the
same nonsense would help.

"WHAT ARE YOU ON ABOUT?" I yelled,

as the house continued to spin.

In the dark I could imagine Will rolling his eyes at me.

"MAGIC!" he shouted.

"WHY DIDN'T YOU JUST SAY SO?" I shouted back, giving him my I-am-not-as-little-as-you-think look.

Water was pretty much everywhere. It was in my ears, in my eyes, in my nose and in my mouth. Thinking back now, I was probably drowning, but at the time I wasn't thinking about that. What I was thinking about was my Auntie Cathy's house. I was thinking about how the mothball smell of her clothes wasn't so bad, even when she hugged you too long. And how I wouldn't even mind if she pinched my cheeks while giving me one of her mossy kisses. And how I might even quite enjoy her mushroom soup if only it meant I wasn't stuck to the side of my house in a pitch-black maelstrom with water in my ears, eyes, nose and mouth.

In short, I was thinking I would rather be anywhere else than where I was.

Then, all of a sudden, I *was* somewhere else, and I was thinking, *Actually I quite miss being stuck to the side of my house.*

ARGHHH!

One moment we were in the water. The next we had been sucked clean through the maelstrom and were flying through mid-air. Flying like a brick.

"ARGHHH!" I said, not for the first time.

"ARGHHH!" replied Will. He's not very original.

It wasn't the falling that worried me. Falling doesn't hurt. It's the ground that hurts – and the ground was getting closer, fast.

"Willllll!" I said, because that's how you sound when you're plummeting through the sky. "Doooooo sooommmethiiing!"

"Liiiiike whaaaaat?" yelled Will.

"Annnnnythiiiiing!"

"Oooookaaaaay. Clooooose yooouuur eeeeeyes!"

"Willlll thaaaaat heeeeelp?" I shouted.

"Nooooo!"

I closed my eyes and waited for the ground.

GLOOP!

When I got to the ground, it wasn't at all how I had imagined it.

For one, it was soft. It was also wet and warm. I'd been expecting to land with a thud or even a bang, but the noise I made was more: *GLOOP!*

The second thing that was surprising was how really, really *stinky* the ground was.

"Am I dead?" I said out loud.

"I don't think so," said Will.

That made me jump, which given recent experience wasn't something I wanted to do again in a hurry. I opened my eyes. "Will, you're alive!"

"We both are," he said.

I was so happy I wanted to leap up and give him a hug. He would've hated it, but I didn't care. I would've hugged him and held on for ages. Only, I couldn't. I couldn't move. I wasn't injured – I hadn't been squashed like a banana in a school bag, or spread thin like peanut butter on bread. I was just stuck. Oh, and did I mention that everything really, really *stank*?

"Will," I said, "what's that smell?"

"Emilie," said Will, "I don't want you to panic."

Do you remember how I said earlier that I hate muckiness? It was No. 3 on the list of things I hate most. Although I'd forgotten about how much I hate rude people, so I guess muckiness should be No. 4, just before big dogs. Anyway, Will wasn't being silly when he said that he didn't want me to panic, because what he said next was exactly the sort of thing that you *would* say if you'd taken a day or so to think very carefully about what to say to make me *completely freak out*.

"I think we might have landed in an enormous poo," said Will. "I think it saved our lives."

"A what?"

"A poo."

"Where?" I said, beginning to panic.

"Ummm," said Will, "everywhere."

I relaxed because I knew he had to be joking.

"Don't be silly," I said. "What in the world could make a poo this big?"

"THAT!" said Will.

Here are five things you should know about dinosaurs:

Things Worth Knowing No. 3
by Emilie

1) Their poos are really big and really smelly.

2) Some of them only ate plants, some of them ate insects and the rest of them would happily have eaten you.

3) The last dinosaurs died about 65 million years ago, so you aren't likely to bump into any.

4) You can ignore No. 3 in this list if you, your brother, your house, a gang of PIRATES and your kidnapped parents were sucked through a huge maelstrom into a lost prehistoric world.

5) Their poos really smell! It's worth saying that twice.

GIGANOTOSAURUS

"What made that noise?" I asked Will.

"A dinosaur," he said very quietly.

"Giganotosaurus, by the sound of it."

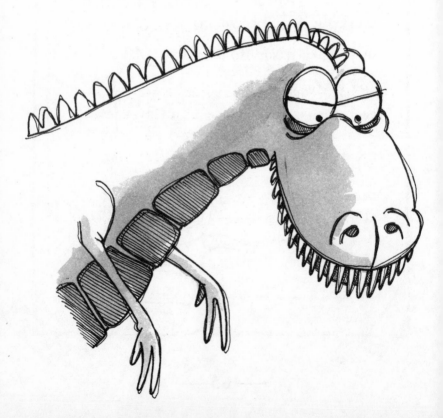

"You made that up," I said. "There is no such thing as a giganotosaurus, or a hugeosaurus or a reallybigoscaryosaurus either."

"Yeah?" said Will. "Tell him that."

OK, just so we are clear, I was wrong about there being no such thing as a giganotosaurus:

RISKYPEDIA
The Adventurer's Encyclopedia

>> GIGANOTOSAURUS

Giganotosaurus (pronounced Jig-a-not-o-saw-rus) was a dinosaur that lived about 97 million years ago in what we now call Argentina. Its name means "giant southern lizard", which makes sense, because it was giant and lived in the south. It basically ate whatever it wanted, because when you are that big, who is going to stop you?

LIZARD LUNCH

The huge lizard (though dinosaurs aren't actually lizards – you can check that if you don't believe me) wandered towards us, sniffing the air. He came closer, and then closer, and then closer still, until his massive nose was poking right into my face, near enough that I could see the tiny scales on his lips. He sniffed deeply and then he roared.

I don't know if you've ever had two express trains speed into your ears, before crashing just behind your eyes.

It's never happened to me. But thanks to that dinosaur, I know what it feels like. My head rang, my eyes shook and my teeth clanked together.

The giganotosaurus's teeth were so close I could see bits of meat trapped between them. He opened his jaws again, wide enough to snap off my head, then wide enough to swallow me whole, and then wider still. And then he sneezed. Huge gobs of dinosaur snot flew all over me.

Then, with a sniffle and a wrinkle of his nose, the dinosaur walked away. I guess we smelt too bad to eat. The poo had saved our lives – again. I'm not happy about that. Being saved by a poo once is embarrassing, but twice? That begins to make that poo some kind of hero.

I looked over at Will and realized he was talking to me. "What?" I said.

I couldn't hear him. I concentrated really hard but his voice was lost behind the roar still rebounding around my head.

"We have to get out of here," said Will in a faraway voice, pointing at something behind me. "The giganotosaurus could come back at any moment and the PIRATES are getting away."

I still couldn't hear him.

"Will," I said, "we have to get out of here. The giganotosaurus could come back at any moment and the PIRATES are getting away."

Will rolled his eyes – he's always doing that – and nodded.

PAN-FRIED PARENTS

It didn't take us too long to spot the
PIRATES. They were making their way
up the side of a distant volcano.

McSnottbeard had Mum over his shoulder.
Dad was tied to a pole being carried by
two members of the **PIRATE** gang.

I felt miserable for my parents, and
for me too, if I'm being honest.

At least my hearing had returned. Then the **PIRATES** began singing and I wished I was still deaf.

"Lug 'em up, lug 'em up,
Lug 'em up to the top of the hill.
Throw 'em in, throw 'em in,
Throw 'em in and watch 'em grill.
Turn 'em over, turn 'em over,
Turn 'em, cook 'em on both sides.
Eat 'em up, eat 'em up,
Eat their innards and their hides."

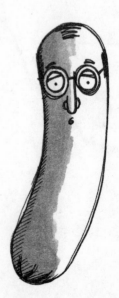

I turned to Will. "They're going to cook our parents!"

"And eat them!" said Will.

An image of Dad as a sausage popped into my head.

Will and I looked at each other for a second, then began sprinting towards the volcano.

TWEET, TWEET, ROAR!

After about five minutes, we began to jog. Then five minutes later we began walking. The volcano was further away than it looked.

"Will," I puffed. "Stop, stop, STOP!"

"What?" said Will, turning around.

"I can't…" I puffed some more. "Too tired, too stinky." I took a deep breath. "I smell like dinosaur poo and the volcano isn't getting any closer. I can't run any more. I can't even walk."

"OK," said Will, looking around.

Then, putting his fingers up to his mouth, he whistled so loud that even the **PIRATES** on the distant volcano stopped to look at us.

"What are you doing?" I asked.

"Calling a dinosaur," said Will.

Here is a little quiz for you:

Test No. 1
by Emilie

When Will told me he was whistling up a dinosaur, did I say:

a) "Good idea, the last dinosaur we met was delightful."

b) "Could you whistle-up my favourite one?"

c) ".............." – nothing?

If you answered C, you got it, because
"................" is exactly what I didn't say. And
then I followed it up with "............!!!!!", which
is what saying nothing looks like when you're
also frantically waving your hands to stop your
brother being dumb.

Will whistled a second time, ignoring me
jumping up and down as I silently begged him
to please, please, please stop.

went something from the other side of some
nearby bushes.

Oh, not again! I thought.

TRIASSIC TRANSPORT

"Quick. I need a rolled-up paper," said Will, confirming he had completely lost his senses.

"OK, I'll just pop down to a prehistoric newsagent's," I replied.

"The map, Emilie! Give me the **PIRATE** map."

I reached into my nightie pocket. Somehow, despite everything that had happened to me, the map was still in there. I handed it to Will, who

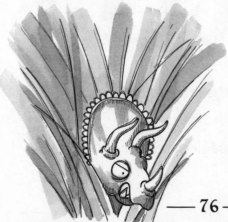

rolled it up and spun to face the bushes just as they burst open to reveal a huge, scaly, three-horned head, which turned out to

be attached to an even huger, scalier body, which was being propelled towards us on four stumpy but still scaly legs.

I took a step back. Will took a step forward. I screamed. The three-horned, four-legged, scaly-all-over monster charged. And Will brought the rolled-up map around in a wide arc and whacked the thing right on its nose.

The dinosaur stopped in its tracks, then backed up on its little legs and began to cry. I guess it had never been smacked on the nose with a rolled-up paper before (given that paper didn't exist when dinosaurs were around) by a boy (given that boys didn't exist) wearing pyjamas (which didn't exist either).

"You're OK," said Will, walking forward and putting his hand on one of the dinosaur's horns before scratching it on the bit where its ear might have been.

"What are you doing?" I asked.

"Getting us a ride," said Will, swinging himself up onto the dinosaur's back. "Hop on."

"Ah – no," I said.

"I thought you couldn't walk any more?"

"That's right," I said. "But I'm still not getting on that. It will eat me."

"It isn't an it," said Will. "It's a triceratops and it won't eat you unless you continue to stand there like a turnip. It's a herbivore."

WHAT MY BROTHER DOES ON TUESDAYS

The triceratops huffed and stamped its feet as Will beckoned to me from its back.

"How do you know so much about dinosaurs?" I asked. "And where did you learn that trick with the rolled-up paper?"

"Oh yeah," Will mumbled. "Well the thing is, I kind of, that is to say, ummm…"

"What?" I said.

"You know how each Tuesday afternoon I have piano practice? Well, that's kind of not really true."

"Not really, as in not at all?" I asked.

"You could say that."

"So what *do* you do on Tuesdays?"

"I train dinosaurs," said Will. "I am kind of a dinosaur trainer. At least, on Tuesday nights I am."

OK, I know that makes no sense.

You're probably thinking, *How can anyone train animals that have been extinct for millions of years?* And if I was lying in a comfortable bed reading this book while my mum and dad wandered around the house occasionally shouting at me to turn the light off and go to sleep, I would think the same thing.

But my bed had been destroyed, along with

the rest of my house. And my parents were
being hauled up a volcano to be cooked by
PIRATES. And I couldn't go to sleep because
there was a triceratops snorting metres away
from me. And on top of all that, if you'd ever
heard Will play the piano, you'd know he'd
never had lessons.

So I did the only thing that seemed sensible
given the circumstances. I hopped on the back of
an animal that hadn't existed for about 65 million
years and held tight as we galloped off to certain
doom at the fiery mouth of an
exploding volcano.

CERTAIN(ISH) DOOM

Here are three things you should know about riding a triceratops:

Things Worth Knowing No. 4
by Emilie

1) Triceratops aren't fast, even when they are galloping.

2) They are hard to stay on, especially when they are galloping.

3) They are hard to stop, particularly once they have started galloping.

Will spent the trip watching the **PIRATES** and digging his heels into the triceratops's ribs to keep it moving along. I spent it holding on as best I could. We didn't talk much. But when we did it went something like this:

"Will?"

"Yep."

"Do you think we'll catch the **PIRATES?**"

"Yep."

"Do you think they're really going to cook our parents?"

"Nope."

"You sure?"

"Nope."

"What are we going to do when we catch up with them?"

"Dunno."

"It's just, there are quite a lot of them."

"Yep."

"And only two of us."

"Yep."

"And one of us isn't very brave."

"OK."

"Do you have a plan?"

"Nope."

"Do you think we *should* have one?"

"Yep."

"Do you want me to be quiet so you can think of one?"

"Yep."

We rode on for a bit.

And then a bit more.

And a bit more.

And a bit more.

And a bit more.

And a bit more.

And a bit more.

And a bit more.

"Do you have a plan yet?" I asked.

"Still nothing," said Will.

We rode on a bit more.

The volcano really was further
away than it looked. In the
distance, I could see
the **PIRATES**
climbing the
smoking
mountain.

A CHANGE OF TRANSPORT

We rode some more.

And then a bit more.

And a bit more.

And a bit more.

And a bit more.

And a bit more.

And a bit more.

"Can't you make this thing go any faster?"
I grumbled to Will. "I think a tortoise just
overtook us."

Will turned to me and smiled. Then he stood up on the back of the triceratops, stared into the sky and let out three loud whistles.

"What are you doing?" I asked.

"Shush," said Will.

There had been way too much shushing lately for my liking. I was about to tell Will just that when something behind me went

"WAAAARK!"

"This should do the trick," said Will, pointing at the sky over my shoulder before tracing his finger down towards the ground.

Something very large thudded onto the ground. Our triceratops snorted unhappily and kind of jigged nervously as it came to a stop.

I turned around very slowly. I didn't expect to see something that would fill me with joy, but I also didn't expect to see something that would make me quite so miserable.

TERRIFYING

I hugged the triceratops a bit tighter.

Sure he was slow and had tried to squash us, but he hadn't once tried to eat me.

I was sure I wouldn't be able to say the same thing about the monster slowly flapping its wings and watching me like you'd watch an ice cream on a hot day.

"Come here girl." Will beckoned to the giraffe-sized horror. It hopped closer.

"What?" I half-screamed. "No, don't come here! Shoo! Go away!"

The thing hopped back and

WAAAAARKed

so loud that wax dropped out of my ears.

"Emilie!" said Will. "Stop that!"

The monster hopped forward a step.

"*You* stop it! That thing's going to eat us!" I screamed, waving my arms.

The thing hopped back.

"No she won't," Will cooed, once again beckoning the bat-giraffe towards us. "And she isn't a *thing*, she's a quetzalcoatlus."

"That isn't even a real word!" I shouted. "It's what you get when you drop a Scrabble board."

I was wrong again.

RISKYPEDIA
The Adventurer's Encyclopedia

>> QUETZALCOATLUS

Quetzalcoatlus (pronounced ket-zel-KWAT-a-lus) was a type of pterosaur, or flying reptile. It may have been the largest animal ever to fly, and with a wingspan of eleven metres could easily carry a child on its back – although under absolutely no circumstances would that be a good idea.

Will shrugged. "She's going to fly us right up to the **PIRATES**," he said.

I had been scared before – now I was petrified.

"What do you mean fly?" I squeaked.

"Fly. Flap. Glide. This is going to be great!"

Will had clearly gone mad. Nuts. Loopy. This wasn't going to be great. It was going to be terrifying.

There was no way I was going to get on the quetzalcoatlus's back.

As it turned out I needn't have worried about that.

"Sorry about this!" yelled Will from his seat between the quetzalcoatlus's shoulder blades. "There really isn't room for both of us up here."

"ARGHHH!" I screamed into the rushing wind as I hung between the quetzalcoatlus's legs.

"I know, it's brilliant isn't it?" shouted Will. "WOOHOO!"

"Not WOOHOO!" I yelled. "ARGHHH!"

"**WAAAAARK!**" screeched the quetzalcoatlus, joining in happily.

"Oh, you can shut up!" I shouted.

TOO LATE

It got hotter as we got closer to the volcano. And smellier – like old eggs that had been stored in someone's armpit.

We swooped in towards the top of the mountain and I caught a glimpse of my parents through the smoke. They were tied in a heap, while at the nearby mouth of the volcano the **PIRATES** were arguing.

"I ain't gonna jump in there," a moustachioed **PIRATE** with two pistols shouted at *McSnottbeard*, as he looked over the edge of the hole.

"Ye don't have to jump. Fallin' in will do thaaar trick," growled the **PIRATE** king, and he shoved the poor man into the smoking pit. The

PIRATE disappeared with a faint scream.

"Anyone else want some help?" *McSnottbeard* sneered and drew his sword, waving it menacingly at his gang.

The remaining **PIRATES** shook their heads, shuffled over to pick up my parents and, reluctantly, trudged to the edge of the volcano mouth.

The quetzalcoatlus dived through a cloud of smoke and straight towards the group. For a brief moment my eyes locked with Mum's. She looked ... scared.

Then the **PIRATES** did the most horrible thing. They tossed my parents into the volcano and, one by one, jumped in after them. We landed on the ledge just as *McSnottbeard* prepared to jump.

"STOP!" I shouted.

McSnottbeard turned. "Go stick yaaar head in a barrel of herring," he growled with a voice that sounded like stones being mixed in a metal bucket. And with that he toppled backwards, arms outstretched, flipping over and out of sight into the volcano.

"NO!" I screamed. "Will, do something!"

But there was nothing to be done. Will slumped off the quetzalcoatlus's back and hit the ground with a thud.

"Will!" I grabbed his arm and pulled him towards me. "They threw Mum and Dad in the volcano!"

Will's face was as white as the smoke all around us.

"Why would they do that?" I asked.

"I don't know," said Will.

"Why?" I implored. "What's the point of stealing someone just so you can jump into a volcano with them?"

"I don't know," he said. "I don't know why they would—" Will leapt to his feet and ran to the volcano's mouth— "jump in with them!" he shouted. And then he began to cry.

MY BROTHER DOESN'T USUALLY CRY

Seeing Will cry was a shock.

It wasn't that Will never cried. Actually he cried quite a lot.

Just a week earlier he had cried for two hours because I swallowed his favourite Lego person (which really wasn't my fault, but that's another story). The thing is, Will didn't usually cry about anything important, because he never really had anything important to cry about.

So it was terrible to see him crying for a real
reason.

Will cried, which made me cry, which
made the quetzalcoatlus happily shout
"WAAAAARK", which just goes to
show you can't rely on dinosaurs to empathize.

The more I watched Will cry, the more I
cried. Only, after a little while, I realized that he
wasn't – wasn't crying, that is.

He was laughing.

BROTHER BABBLE

"Ha!" shouted Will. "You sneaky, stinky **PIRATES**. I should have known!" He ran over, grabbed my arm and dragged me to the mouth of the volcano. My eyes, already filled with tears, began to water from the smoke.

"Look!" Will yelled.

I blinked away huge tears and peered into the boiling pit of molten lava. Or at least that's what I *thought* I was going to look into. What I actually saw was a spinning blue light.

"What's that?" I shouted, as a gust of hot air knocked us back from the edge.

"A wormhole!" Will grabbed me by the shoulder and shook me with joy.

"Must have been a big worm," I said.

"Not a real wormhole." My brother chuckled. "It's a temporal porthole to another place – an Einstein-Rosen bridge!"

RISKYPEDIA
The Adventurer's Encyclopedia

>> WORMHOLES
Wormholes (or Einstein-Rosen bridges) are shortcuts that, in theory, connect two distant points and two different times. Scientists disagree about the possibility that anything could pass through a wormhole without being destroyed, but are unanimous in their opinion that kids would certainly die.

Will was babbling. That's rarely a good sign. Then again, he was smiling and laughing, which was good. But we were standing on the edge of a smoking volcano into which our parents had been thrown, which was bad.

But the fiery belly of the volcano had turned out not to be that fiery after all, which was good.

"You know what this means?" asked Will.

I shook my head.

"We can jump in after the **PIRATES**," he said.

That was really, really bad.

"I'm not jumping anywhere after what happened with that poo!" I shouted over the roar of the volcano.

Will turned to me.

"Emilie," he said, doing his best kind-eyes. "We have to jump. Our parents are in there, or wherever 'in there' leads to."

"But…" I said.

"Emilie," said Will.

"But…"

"Emilie!" shouted Will.

"There's no need to yell," I said.

Will wasn't listening. In fact he wasn't even looking at me any more.

"We *have* to jump!" he shouted again, his

eyes fixed behind me.

"We have to do no such thing!" I said, turning to stare into the face of the giganotosaurus.

It is a fact that giganotosauruses are notoriously rubbish at sneaking up on people.

Here are four reasons why giganotosauruses are rubbish at sneaking up on people:

Things Worth Knowing No. 5
by Emilie

1) Giganotosauruses died out about 97 million years before people existed, so never got much practice.

2) Smart animals tend to be sneaky, and giganotosauruses are about as smart as lettuce.

3) It's hard to sneak when you are thirteen metres long and weigh as much as eight cars.

4) Sneaking doesn't mix well with a deep love of roaring.

And yet, despite all those very valid points, a giganotosaurus had successfully sneaked up behind us.

Right behind us!

"Duck!" yelled Will.

I ducked.

The dinosaur's teeth snapped together where my head had just been.

Will and I scrambled to the edge of the volcano mouth.

"What happens when we jump in?" I shouted.

"If I'm right, we'll be instantly transported to somewhere else, and probably sometime else."

"And if you're wrong?" I asked.

"Probably best not to think about it," he said. "Now, jump!"

And we jumped.

A QUICK TRIP
TO NOWHERE

You are probably wondering what it is like to
fall into a volcano.

I'm still kind of wondering myself. I
remember tumbling. One second I was looking
down into a spinning blue light and the next up
into the disappointed face of a giganotosaurus
watching his lunch disappear.

And then...

Nothing.

Well, not exactly nothing. Will was there.
And I was there. And we were there together,

sitting on the cold stone floor of a small room. We didn't land – there was no bump. And this is going to sound strange, but it felt like we'd been sitting there even before we arrived.

I'm not explaining this very well.

Think of it like this. You know when your parents take you to dinner at one of their friends' houses because they can't get a babysitter? Then when you get there all they do is talk and talk about the dullest things ever, and for so long that you think your brain is going to melt out your ears from boredom?

Eventually you fall asleep on the sofa. And, while you are asleep, your parents pick you up and drive you home. Then the next morning you're a bit surprised to wake up in your own bed, but not really *that* surprised, because even before you woke you knew you were home again.

Well, travelling through a wormhole is like that. It feels quick, but somehow you know it took ages. And once you arrive, you feel like you're where you should be, even if it's a bit surprising to find yourself there.

Only this wasn't at all like waking up in my own bed, because … well, you'll see why in a bit.

DOUBLOONS

"You OK Emilie?" said Will.

"Yeah," I said, thinking that at least we hadn't landed in anything. "Where are we?"

"I don't know," he said, getting up to look around.

The room was lit by huge flaming torches – the old-fashioned type that were meant to be on fire, not battery-powered ones that just happened to be burning. The walls were covered in slime and the slime was covered in little bugs.

"Is there a way out?" I asked.

"There has to be," Will said. "Someone lit these torches, and if they can get in then we can get out."

Will sat down in the middle of the floor.

"What are you doing?" I asked.

"Waiting," he said. "If you have a better plan, I'd be happy to hear it."

I sat next to him until a bug crawled over my hand and I jumped up.

Will sat, and I stood, for a long time. After a while the quiet in the room began to freak me out, so I began talking.

"Will," I said. "Why do you think the **PIRATES** took our parents?"

Will thought for a second, then said, "Probably something to do with doubloons."

I shot Will my "what are you on about?" look, which you'll have realized by now is a crucial part of my communications with my brother.

This is what Riskypedia has to say about doubloons:

"**PIRATES** love doubloons," said Will. "So
maybe they're hoping to sell our parents back to us."

"Will," I said, "we don't have any doubloons."

Our conversation was cut short by a horrible
scraping noise, which resolved itself into a creak
and then the groan of hinges rebelling against a
lack of oil.

"Thith appears to be a little thtuck," said
a cheerful voice as a trapdoor in the ceiling
opened, letting in dim light that mixed lazily
with the gloom in our room.

I looked up to see the most horrid face I had
ever seen giving me the most cheerful smile I
could imagine.

THE IGOR

"Helloooo down there. Everybody OK?" said the face. "Good, good, have you out in a thecond," it added, without waiting for a reply.

Actually, to say it was "a" face is not strictly accurate. It looked very much like a couple of faces stitched together. The left eye had clearly belonged to someone else at some stage; it was maybe twice the size of the right one, which happened to be sewn shut. The ears were stitched on at different angles, so the head looked like it was facing you and looking away at the same time.

"If you hang on just an inthtant, I will get a ladder tho you can climb up," said the patchwork face, before disappearing with a shuffling noise.

"WHAT WAS THAT?!" I whispered in a shouty voice.

"That," said Will, "was an igor."

There was more shuffling.

"Watch out below," the igor shouted. A rope ladder came tumbling through the trapdoor. "Before you come up, I do have to ask one favour. Pleathe, once you are out, don't try to ethcape. There really ith no point."

"OK," said Will, crossing his fingers behind his back. "We won't."

"Oh yeth you will," said the igor. "Our geuthth … our geuththths, our geththth … our vithitors alwayth try to ethcape." The igor smiled again and gave the ladder a little jiggle. "Up you come," he said.

Will held the ladder with one hand and gave it a tug to make sure it was secure. He put a foot on the bottom rung then stopped.

"Just one thing. What happens to us if we don't escape?" Will asked.

"Whatever the Mathter decideth," said the igor.

"The Master?" asked Will.

"Yeth," said the igor. "He ownth this castle."

"And what might he decide?" Will took his foot off the ladder again.

"Dependth on hith mood. Thometimes he liketh to use vithitors for magic practithe, thometimes he feedth our guethth … our geththth … our vithitors to the zombieth. One or the other."

"I see," said Will. "What if we decide to stay down here?"

"I could clothe the hatch again," said the igor. "Thothe little bugth don't like the light. But once the torcheth go out they will come in their thouthan … thouthandth … there will be heapth of them looking for thomething to eat. They can thtrip a perthon to the bone in theconds."

"That's what I thought," said Will, and started to climb. "Come on Emilie, we shouldn't keep the Master waiting."

I followed him up the ladder.

"You know what?" I said as we climbed. "I can't understand a thing that cheerful little man says, but he sure seems nice."

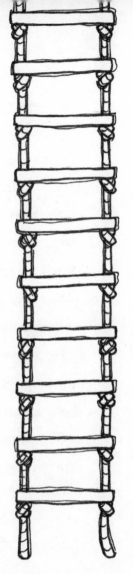

THTITCHES
(WITH AN S)

When I got to the top of the ladder, I saw that we had swapped a gloomy cramped room for a gloomy cramped corridor. The same torches burned on walls made out of the same grey stones covered in the same green slime. At least there were fewer bugs.

The strange little man with the patchwork face gave us a huge smile, then bowed. "Allow

me to introduthe myself. I am Thtitches

Thakths the Thixth, igor to the Count."

"What?" I said.

"Thtitches Thakths," he said, looking a little

nervous. "The Thixth. I am the manthervant to

the Count of—"

"Nope," I said. "I can't understand a thing

you're saying."

The smile on his face disappeared.

"It'th thith tongue," he said. "I have only had it

for a few days. It belonged to my couthin, Thethil

Thakths. I inherited it along with hith good eye."

The igor pointed to the eye that wasn't closed.

"The eye workth great but the tongueth no good

at etheth."

"Etheth?" I said.

"Yeth," he said gloomily. "It maketh it terribly

difficult to thay my name."

"Your name?" I said.

"Yeth, my name."

"Your name is Yeth?" I smiled encouragingly.

The igor shook his head.

"It's not Yeth, is it?" I said. "Oh, I wish I could understand you. You were so nice to get us out of that horrible little room."

Sometime during the conversation Will had started tapping his head against the wall and groaning.

"Stop that Will," I said. "You'll get a sore head."

"I already have a sore head," he said. "Look Emilie, his name is Stitches Saks the Sixth. He's the igor, which is kind of like a butler built from spare parts, to whoever owns this castle. He can't pronounce the letter 's' because he recently got a new tongue. And he hasn't saved us from anything. He's going to hand us to his master, who will probably feed us to some zombies."

I looked over at the igor, who was grinning

from ear to ear at being understood.

"Oh be quiet," I said to Will. "You don't have any idea what he's saying either." Then turning to the igor I said, "If you would please show us the way out, we will be on our way. We have to get our parents back from some **PIRATES**."

I took Yeth's hand. He pulled away a little at first, but I held on tight until he relaxed and we set off down the corridor.

A FEW THINGS ABOUT IGORS

I was wrong of course. Yeth's name wasn't Yeth. It was Stitches, like Will said. And I was eventually fed to some zombies, so you should prepare yourself for some more screaming.

Here are five things you should know about igors:

Things Worth Knowing No. 6
by Emilie

1) Igors aren't born – they are made. They are stitched together from bits of other igors and they regularly add new

bits as the old ones wear out. They are always changing, but only so they can more or less stay the same.

2) Igorth alwayth thpeak like thith. It's because their tongues don't fit terribly well.

3) Igors are really rather nice and helpful.

4) But that doesn't mean they do nice things. You see, every igor has a master and will do whatever they ask them to do.

5) Igors' masters are never nice and definitely not helpful.

WILL?

We walked down the corridor, around a corner, then down another corridor. Then down a hallway, around a bend and down another hallway.

As we walked, Yeth and I held hands and chatted. He wasn't much of a walker – his legs came from different relatives – but we had a great talk (even if I didn't understand most of what he said).

In fact, we were having such a good time chatting we forgot all about Will, and by the time we remembered him he was gone.

"Oh no," said Yeth.

I was stunned. "Do you think he escaped?" I asked Yeth. "He said he wouldn't. Then again, you can't trust my brother. Do you know he doesn't go to football training or piano lessons?"

Yeth held up his hand and shook his head.

"No more talking," he said. "It is time to meet the Mathter."

And with that, Yeth knocked on a huge double door.

* A brief note before we meet the Master
The story gets extra scary for a bit. I thought I would warn you just in case you were planning on reading this next chapter just before you go to sleep. I wouldn't, if I was you.

IN THE ROOM

The big wooden doors swung open with a groan. I looked into the room. Or at least I looked in as much as I could. It was dark in there.

The walls were as high as a two-storey house. On one side they were covered in thick red curtains that filtered the thin sunlight into a soupy blood colour.
Along the other walls were tapestries, almost all of them featuring pointy-eared men with equally pointy noses.

In the centre of the room was a heavy wooden table, on which a candle sat flickering in a skull. Behind the table

was a chair and in the
chair was ... well, no one.

The room felt empty, and
I don't mean just empty of
people – it felt empty of
everything. There was no
noise. None. It was so quiet I
could hear the blood pumping
in my ears. It was pumping
pretty hard.

"Hello?" I said as quietly
as I could, as I stepped into
the room. "Anyone there?"

"Yesssss?" said a voice that seeped slowly out
from all the dark places in the room.

"Is that you Yeth?" I asked.

"Nooooo." The voice slid around the walls
until it slithered into place behind me. I spun
around to face the door. No one was there.

"Where are you?"

"I am not hiding," said the voice, slippery and

dry and from just behind me.

I spun around again. I was getting a bit dizzy to tell the truth.

What I saw this time nearly made me scream.

OK, I screamed.

Sitting at the table was the most horrifying man I'd ever had the misfortune to lay my eyes on.

He was tall and incredibly thin. His face was long and sharp, cut horizontally with thin eyes that held coal-black pupils. Below his dagger-point of hair was an equally pointy nose that sat above a thin mouth punctuated by long fangs. The fangs of a snake, I thought.

"Vhat have ve here then?" said the man.

"It's a little girl, a vee little girl who screams. And vhat I am asking myself is, vhy is this noisy little girl in my castle?"

He looked and sounded like a snake, but his attitude was all tiger. He watched me, barely moving except for the occasional twitch of his long, thin fingers.

"Vhat are you calling yourself?" he asked me in that strange voice that came from everywhere at once. I opened my mouth but couldn't speak. There was something about him that meant, even as he stared right at you, you didn't want to do anything more to attract his attention.

"I'm Emilie," I squeaked.

"Meez Emilie." He rolled my name around in his mouth as if he could taste it. "Vell, Meez Emilie, I am ze great Count Salazar. And I vould like to say velcome to my castle."

"Thank you," I whispered.

"I had not finished," Salazar snapped. "I vas going to say, I vould *like* to say velcome to my castle, but indeed you are *not* velcome. You are intruding."

"I found her in the dungeon," said the igor, who seemed to have appeared from nowhere. "Her and her brother."

"Twoooo intruders?" said Salazar. A flicker of anger passed over his face. "Now I am vondering, if there are two children intruding in my castle, vhy am I seeing only one?"

A FEW THINGS ABOUT ZOMBIES

Count Salazar isn't a zombie. But some zombies come along in a bit and I thought I would break up the tension a little by telling you about them now. You know things are bad when talking about zombies eases the tension.

Here are five things you should know about zombies:

Things Worth Knowing No. 7
by Emilie

1) Zombies aren't alive, but they aren't exactly dead either – this is as confusing

to them as it probably is to you.

2) Zombies smell. Then again, everything in this story smells.

3) Zombies kill and eat people, and not necessarily in that order.

4) If a zombie bites you and doesn't kill you, then you become a zombie.

5) And the last thing (and this is something I really wish I had known): there are a bunch of them just beneath a trapdoor that is just beneath me at this point in the story.

SOME OTHER THINGS I WISH I'D KNOWN

There are three things I wish I'd known as I stood in that room. The first was that I was standing on a trapdoor. The second was that under that trapdoor was a whole shamble of zombies. The third was where my brother was.

Count Salazar knew the first two things. And it turned out he was rather keen to discover the third.

"Vhere is this brother?"

I didn't say anything. I had no idea where Will was. So I shrugged.

"Vhat is that?!" Salazar shouted, as he stuck

out his bottom lip and shrugged. "Ve answer vith vords vhen ze great Count Salazar asks a question! Ve do not shrug. Do you understand?!"

I nodded, then thought better of it. "Yes," I said.

"Good," said Salazar, lowering his voice again. "Vhere is your brother?"

Salazar's attitude was beginning to annoy me.

"I ... DON'T ... KNOW," I said, with a pause in between each word. "IF ... YOU ... ARE ... SO ... GREAT ... YOU ... FIND ... HIM."

"Oh ... ve *vill* find him," sneered Salazar.

It was meant to be a threat, but I was too annoyed to be scared.

"Bet you don't," I said. "Will is really good at hiding."

That's true by the way. Once I didn't find him for almost a day. Admittedly I didn't try that hard. Also it turned out Will had hidden in a cupboard and couldn't get out. He was really hungry by the time someone heard him shouting.

"Perhaps he is good at ze hiding," said

Salazar. "Perhaps he is soooo good that no person could ever find him. But I have something better than persons."

All the time he was talking he was smiling. It started to make me nervous.

"Igor," said Salazar. "Release ze werewolves!"

"The werewolveth, Mathter?" asked Yeth.

"Yes," said Salazar. "The werewolves!"

"Really?" said Yeth.

"Yes."

"Do I have to?"

"Yes."

"OK," Yeth said with a sigh, as he turned to hobble out the door.

"This is your last chance," said Salazar. "Tell me vhere your brother is hiding. Once ze werewolves are released they vill hunt until they have found their prey. Then they vill devour him."

I was horrified. But what could I do? I didn't know where Will was. I didn't even know enough about the castle to *lie* about where he might be. But that didn't stop me.

"He's in the pink room," I said.

OK, clearly there wasn't going to be a pink room in this grim castle. If I had my time again I would have chosen another colour. Brown would have been better. Grey might have worked. But pink? Pink was ridiculous!

"Ze pink room?" said Salazar.

"Yes," I said.

"Ve don't have a pink room."

"Yes you do."

"No, I am quite sure ve don't."

"We walked past it on the way here."

"You valked past a pink room?"

"Pretty sure."

"It's impossible."

"Are you sure?" I asked. "It's a big castle. Have you been in all the rooms?"

"Vell, not all of them, I guess I could have missed one…" Salazar paused and then shouted, "No! No! No! Ve do not have a pink room! This is a castle of horrors, and castles of horrors do not have pink rooms!"

"Maybe it was light red?" I said, but Salazar wasn't listening any more.

He stood. He was enormously tall. "Release ze werewolves!" he screamed in a voice that echoed around the room.

There was a shuffling outside the door and I heard a terrible howl.

"GAAAAAARRRRRROOOOOOTH!"

A terrible, yet kind of familiar, howl.

"What was that?" I asked.

"The werewolves!" roared Salazar. "They are hunting!"

"HOOOOOOOOWWWWWLLLLTH!" went the noise from just outside the door.

"That doesn't sound much like a wolf," I said.

"Yes it does," said Salazar.

"It sounds a bit like Yeth," I said.

"Vhat?" said Salazar, looking unsure for the first time since I'd met him.

"That sounds like Yeth, standing just outside the door pretending to be a wolf."

"Does not," said Salazar.

"Yes it does," I insisted. "You can hear the 'TH' noise at the end of each howl."

I turned to the door. "Do it again Yeth," I shouted.

"It is werewolves, not Yeth – I mean, my igor," hissed Salazar.

"No it's not. It's you, isn't it Yeth?"

"NOOOOOOOOOOOOOOOOOOOO!" came a howl from behind the door.

I began to giggle. "You don't even have werewolves, do you?"

"Yes I do," said Salazar.

"Then why is Yeth howling?" I was laughing quite hard now.

"Stop laughing," the Count shouted.

But I couldn't. I was imagining Yeth with a little tail and sad puppy-dog ears.

"Stop!" Salazar shouted again.

"Make me." I giggled.

That, as it turns out, is the wrong thing to say to a warlock.

"OK," hissed the Count, and with a flick of his hand and a word I didn't quite catch, I froze.

WARLOCK, WITCHES AND PIRATES

You might have noticed back there that I mentioned something new about Salazar. Perhaps you didn't. So I'll say it again: Salazar is a warlock.

That's a kind of male witch, only not really. You see, witches are quiet, kind women who own slightly too many brooms and know the sort of magic that is mostly used to cure things like gassy tummies. Warlocks, on the other hand, are never nice. The magic they know does horrible things and they have no idea how to treat a gassy tummy. I probably should have told you about them earlier – only I didn't know Salazar was a warlock until he froze me stiffer than an ice cube in a freezer in the snow on a glacier at the North Pole.

Oh, and one more thing about warlocks: they spend a lot of time hanging around with **PIRATES**.

I smelt the **PIRATES** before I heard them. And, unfortunately, I heard them before I saw them. They were singing again.

> *"There's nothing smellier than me,*
> *Not a farty old dog or a wee.*
> *Not a dead fish in the sun*
> *Or manure by the tonne,*
> *No, there's nothing smellier than me.*

There's nothing scarier than I,
Not a finger in a meat pie.
Not a bump in the dark
Or a hammerhead shark,
No, there's nothing scarier than I.

There's nothing nastier than us,
Not a scab on your knee full of pus.
Not a slug on your tongue
Or this song what we sung,
No, there's nothing nastier than us."

"NgGGGmMnf!" I yelled when I saw the
PIRATES – which is what screaming
sounds like when you're frozen.

That first scream was out of fear. The next
was out of happiness.

"NgGGGmMnf!" I shouted, because Mum
was there.

"NgGGGmMnf!" replied Mum, who was
slung over one of the **PIRATES'** shoulders
with tape over her mouth.

I saw Dad next. He was still strung up
on a pole between two **PIRATES**. I
"NgGGGmMnf!"-ed all over again with joy.

"ZZZ-zz-hgngh-zz," said Dad, which is more
or less the noise all dads make when they are
sleeping.

Dads can fall
asleep in any
circumstances.

OFF WITH MY HEAD

"Arrrr," said *McSnottbeard* when he saw me. **PIRATES** start every sentence with "Arrrr", and end most sentences the same way. I'll leave the "Arrrr"s out from now on.

"Slap me with an octopus! If it ain't the wee fish fart what's been followin' us all day." *McSnottbeard* walked over to me. The smell was horrendous. "I thought we'd lost ye back at the volcano. Actually, I thought we'd lost ye back at the house, then at the whirlpool, then in the dinosaur world, and then at the volcano. But here ye are again."

If I'd been able to speak, I would've corrected him about the whirlpool being a maelstrom.

"Well you'll not be followin' us any longer," said *McSnottbeard*, drawing his cutlass. "I'm gonna cut your noggin off."

The **PIRATE** strode towards me, raising his cutlass to head height – specifically, my head's height.

"Gmfff!" came a muffled shout from Mum.

McSnottbeard stopped and turned to look at her.

"Nae the noggin?" he asked.

Mum shook her head.

"The legs?"

"Gmfff...!" grunted Mum.

"Arrrr," the **PIRATE** huffed. "Yaaar ruinin' all the fun!"

Yeth shuffled up beside *McSnottbeard*. The igor had a peg on his nose.

"Everything ith ready Mathter Mcthnottbeard," he said. "You and your friendth can leave now ... pleathe."

"Eeeeuw!" shouted *McSnottbeard*. "What

happened to yaarrr face?"

Yeth ignored him. "The portal ith ready."

McSnottbeard shook his head. "No. I cannae
understand a word ye are sayin'," he said.
"Perhaps I could chop your noggin off ... but it
looks like someone beat me to it."

Salazar gently wafted his hand in front of his nose. "Enough with ze head chopping. It is time you and your stench – sorry, gang – left."

The warlock walked to a wall and traced a rectangle with his finger. The wall inside the rectangle glowed then disappeared into a blue light.

"Abracadabra!" Salazar said with a flourish.

"Mighty impressive," said *McSnottbeard*. "Come on lads, let's get on arrrrr way."

The **PIRATES** began to shuffle towards the magic door when Salazar clicked his fingers and they froze.

"Before you go," Salazar said, gliding over to *McSnottbeard*, "there vas that small matter of payment."

"Gmfffmaaar," growled *McSnottbeard*.

Salazar tutted at the **PIRATE**. "You remember our agreement? I send you back to your island, and you give me fifty doubloons."

The warlock reached into the **PIRATE**'s

pocket and lifted out a bag of coins. Then, stepping back, he flicked his hand and released the **PIRATES**. *McSnottbeard* spun around with a roar, his sword extended towards Salazar.

"I could freeze you again," said the warlock. "Some **PIRATE** statues around ze castle vould add to ze spookiness."

McSnottbeard lowered his cutlass. "Just make sure that wee prawn-poop doesn't follow us nay-more."

And with that, the **PIRATES** walked through the wall, taking my parents with them.

THINGS COULD
BE WORSE

The moment the **PIRATES** were gone, the magic door flashed and disappeared with a noise like a zip closing. The wall was just a wall again.

"Thank goodness that is over," said Salazar, as Yeth appeared at his side with a mop and bucket. "Igor, please clean the ... oh good."

"The thmell ith unbearable," said Yeth, ringing out his mop and removing the peg from his nose.

"Now vhere vas I?" said Salazar. "Oh yes."

With a wave of his hand Salazar unfroze me. I slumped to the ground and began rubbing my legs, which tingled as the blood returned.

Normally in bad situations I find it helpful to remind myself that things could be worse. The problem was that just at that moment I couldn't really imagine *how*. But that was only because I still didn't know that I was lying on a trapdoor above a cave full of zombies. I guess if I'd known about the zombies I might have thought to myself, *Well, at least I haven't been dropped into the pit full of flesh-eating monsters.* That might have cheered me up a little.

But not for long.

"You will leave us now, Meez Emilie," said Salazar. And with a flick of his wrist the trapdoor opened up beneath me.

THE PIT

I plunged into darkness as black as the inside of a squash ball. Plunged for about a second, that is, before I hit the ground.

"Ouch," I said, rubbing a knee.

"Oooooch," went something from the darkness in the cave.

That was probably just an echo, I thought to myself.

"Hello," I said to the darkness.

"Helloooooo, helloooo, helloooo," the darkness said back.

See, just an echo.

"Dinnerrrr," went the darkness.

Oh cripes, I thought to myself. *The echo is hungry.* Then something moved. *Oh double-*

cripes, the echo is hungry and moving.

I squinted and looked into the darkness. I looked way, way, way, way into the darkness.

And as I looked, a pair of eyes suddenly opened just in front of me.

"Arrrrrrrrrrrrgh!" I shouted, squirming back against a wall.

"Urgggghhhhhh!" responded whatever was attached to the eyes.

I couldn't make out who owned the eyes, so I blinked hard, squeezing my eyes shut to get used to the dark. When I opened them again, two pairs of eyes were staring back at me.

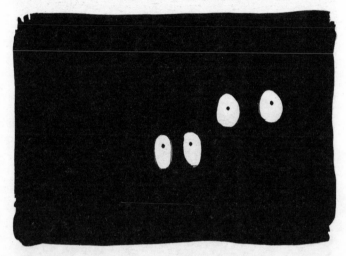

Then a third pair joined the second.

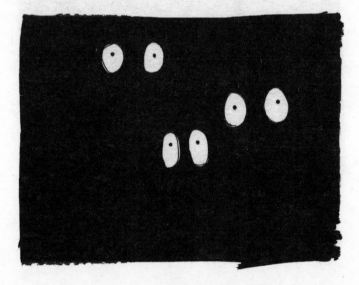

And then a fourth pair joined the third.

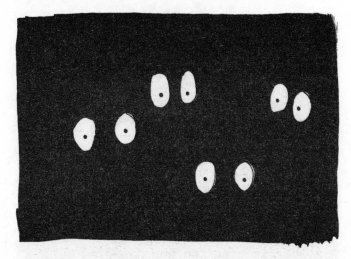

And then – well, you get the idea.

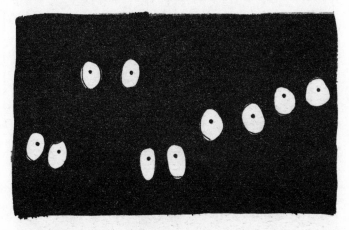

"Dinnnnnerrrr," the crowd of eyes said, and they began to edge forward.

NO ESCAPE

RISKYPEDIA
The Adventurer's Encyclopedia

>> ZOMBIE
A zombie is a person who has died but doesn't seem to realize it. Anyone bitten by a zombie will turn into a zombie. That's mainly a problem because zombies love eating people. In fact, the only thing zombies love more than human flesh is human brain, which is hardly a consolation.

I tried to scramble away but my back was already against the wall. I looked up to see if there was any way out, but the trapdoor was too high.

This time, when I looked back into the cave, I could make out the owners of the eyes, though I wished I couldn't. In front of me were five zombies, one for each pair of eyes. Their faces were green and hairless, with a thin covering of dry skin. In their black mouths were grey teeth, but not many. They staggered, as if constantly surprised to find the ground meeting their feet.

"Dinnnnnerrrrr," they said, as their hands grasped at the air in front of me. I curled myself into a ball, lifting my knees up to my chest and hooking my arms over the top of my head. A braver person might have fought, but I am

evidently not that brave. *They eat brains,* I thought to myself. *Zombies eat brains.* I tucked my head in tighter.

I closed my eyes as the first flat, hard hand slapped down on my shoulder. A second hand beat down on my thigh. Then hands pressed down all over me. They were rough and strong, and stung as they hit my skin. *This is it,* I thought as the hands lifted me off the ground.

"Emilie, Emilie, Emilie," the zombies mumbled to each other.

Hang on, I thought, as I was carried back into the darkness to be eaten. *How do they know my name?*

Then suddenly the carrying stopped and I was dumped onto my feet.

"Hello Emilie," a familiar voice said from the dark.

VEGEZOMBIANS

Here are five things I didn't expect to see in the cave:

Things I Didn't Expect to See No. 1
by Emilie

1) Will

2) Will

3) Will

4) Will

5) A huge pile of carrots

OK, I know that's really only two things, but I was really surprised to see my brother.

"Will!" I shouted, and ran to give him a hug. I stopped two steps short. "Are you a zombie? Did they bite you and turn you into a zombie?"

"No, Emilie, I am not a zombie," Will replied.

"How do I know?" I took a step back, then remembered all the zombies still behind me and took a step forward again. "If I was a zombie and wanted to eat someone I would definitely say I *wasn't* a zombie. Then when the person gave me a hug, CHOMP! I'd have their brains for afternoon tea."

Will rolled his eyes. "I'm not a zombie. And I don't want you to hug me."

"It really *is* you!" I rushed the last few steps to give him a huge hug.

"Urgh," groaned Will. "Get off me."

I held on even tighter as the questions tumbled out of me. "Why did you run away? How did you get down here? How did you survive without getting eaten by *them*?" I pointed to the zombies, who were shuffling closer to us again. "Why aren't they eating us now? Are they going to eat us in a bit? Did you know that I saw *McSnottbeard*? And Mum and Dad? And that there's a man up there who sounds like a snake but acts like a tiger?"

"Do you want me to answer *all* of that?" asked Will.

I nodded.

He disentangled himself from my hug and held up his fist.

"I ran away so I could come back and save you." He flicked a finger up with each answer. "I walked here. I haven't been surviving down here, I've been waiting for you. They aren't eating us because they are *vege*zombians. Because they are *vege*zombians, they are not going to eat us later." Will lifted up his second fist and continued flicking up fingers. "I heard *McSnottbeard* speaking to you. I heard Mum grunting. I think I heard Dad snoring. That man is Count Salazar, and he is more of a lizard and a pussycat than a snake and a tiger. Is that everything?"

I nodded again.

"Can we go now?" he asked.

"Ummm…" I said, putting my hands up, palms outward in the international sign for STOP. "*What* is a *vege*zombian?"

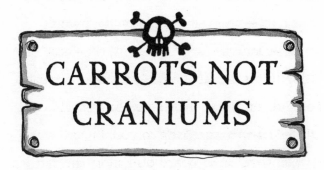

CARROTS NOT CRANIUMS

A *vege*zombian, it turns out, is a zombie that has given up eating people, to pursue a healthier diet – mostly carrots and lettuce.

RISKYPEDIA
The Adventurer's Encyclopedia

>> VEGEZOMBIANS
The first vegezombians appeared in the mid-1300s, probably as a result of a people-shortage caused by the Black Plague (though possibly because of a misunderstanding surrounding the term "head of lettuce").

I am not saying I wasn't grateful for the zombies'

dietary choices, but given the option of people or vegetables for the rest of my life, I would probably starve.

"Will," I said, "if the zombies were never going to eat me then what was all that 'dinnnnerrrr' nonsense?"

"Oh, that," said Will, pointing to the carrots. "I promised them these if they saved you."

"Dinnnnerrrr," moaned the zombies as they staggered past Will towards the root vegetables.

"Whoa guys," said Will. "First you get us out, *then* carrots."

The zombies groaned. Zombies are always groaning. Then they shuffled towards the trapdoor. Zombies are always shuffling too. They lined up one behind the other, before the first one lay down. Then the second one got on its hands and knees. The third crouched. The fourth stood, as did the fifth, though it raised its hands above its head.

"What is that?" I asked.

Will started walking towards the zombies. "Stairs," he said. "Shall we get going?"

He stepped on the first zombie, then the second, and step-by-step, or zombie-by-zombie, climbed out of the pit.

MOPS AND MATHTERS

When I got back in the room, Yeth was swinging his mop at Will.

"The Mathter won't be happy," he mumbled, jabbing his soapy weapon at my brother. "You were meant to have run away. And you —" Yeth swung his mop towards me, spraying mucky water all over my nightie (I bet you'd forgotten I was still in my nightie) — "You were thuposed to have been zombie-lunch."

And then, with a puff of smoke, the Count appeared in all his snake-like horror.

Oh, and he was in a bath towel and holding a rubber ducky.

"Igor, have you seen ze shampoo? Mr Quackenstein and I are going to have a bath," he said, holding up his duck.

Yeth shuffled uncomfortably. "Mathter. We have getht-th … getht … the people are back."

Salazar, who had been looking at his duck, lifted his eyes to look at Yeth. "Vhere?"

Yeth pointed his mop at us.

Salazar turned, bared his fangs and hissed.

My knees gave way.

And then, well, Will took a step forward. "Hello Milo," he said with a cheerful wave. "So this is your castle, is it?"

WHAT MY BROTHER DOES ON WEDNESDAYS

Salazar looked at Will.

Will looked at Salazar.

I looked at Yeth.

Yeth shrugged his shoulders and went back to mopping the floor.

"What are you doing?" I whispered to Will.

"Saying hi to an old friend," Will said with a smile.

OK, I know I shouldn't have been surprised. But just because your brother turns out to be a **PIRATE**-hunting, dinosaur-training vegezombian expert, doesn't mean you'd expect him to be on a first-name basis with a warlock who just tried to feed you to his pet monsters.

"Friend?" I asked.

"Milo and I have known each other since year one."

"Year one of *what*?!" I was shouting a little.

"Oh, that," Will mumbled. "Well the thing is, I kind of, that is to say, ummm … you know how each Wednesday I have art classes after school?"

"Not again?"

"Yeah." Will nodded. "Milo and I take wizardry lessons together."

HOW I ALMOST BECAME A MONKEY

Salazar, or Milo, if you prefer, smiled a huge but still horrifying smile.

"How are you Villiam?"

"Tired," said my brother. "It's been a long day."

"Is this your sister vhat is alvays breaking your Lego?"

Will nodded.

"I see vhat you mean about her being annoying."

"Hey!" I yelled, but no one was paying any attention to me.

"Do you vant that I should turn her into a slug?"

"You can do that?" asked Will.

"It isn't difficult," said Salazar, as he stepped forward and put his arm around Will. "Or perhaps a monkey? It's easier, there is less to change."

"You can't turn me into a monkey!" I shouted.

"Ve can." Salazar nodded at Will.

"No you can't!" I screamed.

Salazar looked confused. "Sure ve can. Ve'd need a few things for ze spell: gunpowder, frogs' eyes, snakes' blood, some maple syrup. Ze syrup is for ze taste."

"I don't want to be a monkey," I said to Will.

Will shrugged, then turning to Salazar said, "Maybe another time. Right now we need your help catching those **PIRATES**."

Will and the Count wandered off to the far side of the room, their hands on each other's shoulders, their heads close together as they talked.

I was thinking it might not be so bad being a monkey, when I noticed my foot was wet. I looked down to find it covered in a mop held by a smiling and nervous-looking Yeth.

"Hello," I said, giving him a pat on his bald head.

"I am glad you weren't conthumed," he said.

"What?"

"Thnacked upon."

"What?"

"Ingethted … by the zombieth."

I shook my head.

"Finithed off." Yeth began to look a little desperate.

I patted him again. "You really are a dear little man, even if you are impossible to understand. You know, I don't think you wanted to feed me to the zombies at all."

Yeth smiled.

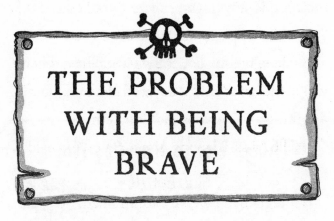

THE PROBLEM WITH BEING BRAVE

I already mentioned that I am not very brave. I'm not ashamed to say that. Some kids will do anything to prove they are brave. Not me. Brave kids end up with broken arms and bloody knees. Brave, you see, isn't always just brave – it can be stupid, too. And I may not be brave but I'm not stupid either.

The dumbest kid in my school is Murray Merkinson. Some people think he's the bravest too. Murray will do anything to prove he isn't chicken. He once bit the head off a cockroach, just because someone said he wouldn't. He had to go home sick afterwards.

I think that anyone willing to bite the head off a live cockroach is probably already sick.

Here are the top five things you'll hear when you're being asked to do something really dumb:

Things Worth Knowing No. 8
by Emilie

1) I dare you.

2) Are you chicken?

3) It won't hurt.

4) I did it.

5) It will be fun.

You might want to copy that list out and keep it handy. That way if your brother and a warlock ever walk over to you with big smiles on their faces and suggest you should jump through a magic portal, you'll know exactly what to say.

"We have to go after Mum and Dad and this is the quickest way," said Will, motioning to a portal that Salazar had just magicked onto the wall. "Actually it's the only way. It'll be fun."

(No. 5 on the list!)

"No," I said. "It won't be fun. It'll be horrible and dangerous."

"It won't hurt," said Will (No. 3 on the list!). "You step in here and then straight back out on the other side."

"And how do I know what's *on* the other side?" I asked. "I might end up in another dungeon! Or dinosaur poo! Or right next to *McSnottbeard*!"

Will looked across at Salazar.

"Actually, that is exactly vhere you vill end up," said the Count. "This is ze same spell I used to send ze **PIRATES** back to their hideout. You aren't chicken, are you?"

(No. 2 on the list!)

"Cluck," I said.

"C'mon," said Will. "I dare you."

"It isn't dangerous," chimed in Salazar. "I have done it plenty of times."

"No. 1 *and* No. 4!" I shouted.

Will sighed. "You can stay here if you want."

"I can?" I was a little shocked.

"Why not?" said Will. "Milo can bring you along to next Wednesday's wizardry class. I'll take you home afterwards, assuming we still *have* a home and the **PIRATES** haven't killed me."

Obviously I was going to go with him. If I stayed, I'd be turned into a monkey quicker than you can say bananas. Also, I couldn't really let Will go on his own. He'd get killed. Or worse, save everyone all by himself.

That wouldn't really be worse, but it would be bad. Will would probably get extra ice cream for ever. I would have to eat double portions of beans.

So I did the only thing I could do. I stepped
through the portal.

WISH YOU WERE HERE

The end of that last chapter was a little ominous, so you're probably expecting this chapter to start with something horrible, in which case this next bit is going to be a let-down.

I stepped through the wall and straight out onto a rather nice tropical beach.

The sand was warm beneath my feet. The water was clear, with a hint of green, just the way I'd seen it in holiday magazines.

The sun shone through a sky smudged with thin clouds and behind me palm trees waved in a gentle wind.

I suddenly felt very tired. *It would be nice to have a deckchair,* I thought. And no sooner

had I thought it than I noticed a chair just
a few metres up the beach. "Yes," I said to
myself, as I sat down. I was asleep in seconds.
Unfortunately, I was awake seconds after that.

"Wake up Emilie," said Will, nudging my
shoulder.

"I don't wanna go to school today," I
mumbled, swatting him away.

"OK. You don't have to."

"Good," I said, and rolled over. I lay there for
a bit as my sleepy brain caught up with the past
few hours.

"Will," I said.
"There's no school
today, is there?"

"Nope."

"Instead of
school," I groaned,
"are we going to
be storming the
secret hideout of

a band of ruthless **PIRATES** in a hopeless bid to get our parents back?"

"Yep."

"I think I'd like to go to school after all," I said as I opened my eyes.

Will was sitting next to me on another deckchair. He looked very relaxed.

"It's nice here," I said.

"Yeah, really nice," Will replied, lying back in his deckchair and stretching out his legs. "It's not real of course," he added.

TRAPPED

I looked around at the beach, the water and the palm trees, and then back at Will.

"Which bit's not real?" I asked.

"All of it," Will replied. "It's a trap."

"Is it?" I was a little confused. "It's a nice trap. Better than the zombie pit."

"That's what makes it so cunning," said Will. "It's a magic trap. A wizard called Mungo invented it."

"That's not much of a name for a wizard," I said.

Will ignored me.

"Mungo was Scottish. Miserable place Scotland – at least it is on a rainy winter's day, and Mungo hated rain and winter more

than most. So he created a spell
to transform any place into a
paradise that exactly suits the
person in it.

"It worked brilliantly.
So brilliantly that
Mungo never left home
again."

"What happened to
him?" I asked.

"Nothing," Will
replied. "As far as
anyone knows he's
still at home, he just
never answers the door. That's what makes this
trap so dangerous. In most traps people stay
because they can't get out. In this trap people
stay because they don't want to leave."

FIZZ AND
FRANKFURTERS

I looked around the beach again. I didn't want to
leave.

"So all I have to do is wish for something and it
will appear?" I asked.

Will nodded.

"I wish we had some lemonade." No sooner
had the words left my mouth than I was holding
a large glass of sparkling lemonade with a little
umbrella in it. Will had one too.

"Oh this is cool," I squealed. I took a long sip
of my drink. It tasted like bubbles of happiness. I
sat back and closed my eyes. "Will," I said. "If we
can wish for anything, why don't we just wish for
Mum and Dad?"

Will shook his head. "The trap is still just a trap. It only works on people who walk into it."

"That's a pity," I said, pushing my toes into the warm sand. "Should we get some snacks?"

A plate of frankfurters, the tiny ones that come on sticks, appeared. Will shook his head. The sausages disappeared.

"We have to go," he said. "It's dangerous here. The longer we stay, the harder it'll be to leave."

I groaned. "Which way?"

"Let's find out," said Will, getting up out of his chair and walking down to the water. "I wish we had a map."

A bottle immediately washed up on the sandy beach.

Will uncorked the bottle and pulled out a rolled-up map. He walked back and sat down next to me.

"We are here." He pointed to the map.

"How do you know?" I asked.

"There's a picture of both of us sitting on deckchairs," said Will.

I looked at the map. There in the corner was Will holding the map and me looking over at it. We were moving too. I lifted my drink to my lips and map-me did the same thing.

"Cool!" I said. "So what else is there?"

We looked at the map again. You can look now, if you like. It's on the next page.

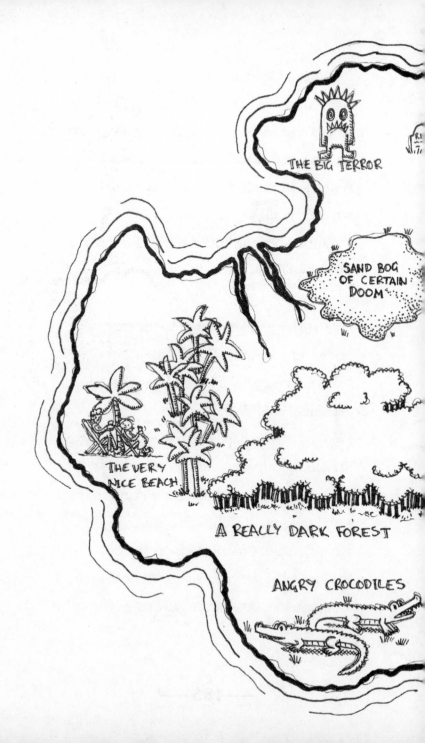

THE BIG TERROR

SAND BOG
OF CERTAIN
DOOM

THE VERY
NICE BEACH

A REALLY DARK FOREST

ANGRY CROCODILES

PIRATE
GRAVEYARD

N
W   E
S

PIRATE BAY
PARKING

PIRATE HIDEOUT

SKULL-FACE ROCK—
BECAUSE THERE
IS ALWAYS
A SKULL-FACE ROCK

PICNIC AREA

NO
SWIMMING

MAGIC MAP

The first thing you might notice is that we are on the other side of the island from the thing marked "**PIRATE** HIDEOUT". The second thing worth noting is the huge, really dark forest in the middle of the map. I knew straight away it was a really dark forest, because on the map it said "A REALLY DARK FOREST".

"I don't much like the look of that forest," I told Will.

We looked to the bottom of the map. There were crocodiles – "ANGRY CROCODILES" – according to the map.

"I don't like the look of them either," Will said. He pointed at the crocodiles, which immediately started snapping at his finger.

"What about the other side?" I said, pointing towards something called the "SAND BOG OF CERTAIN DOOM".

Will touched the map where the bog was and his finger sank straight in.

"Urgggh," said Will, snatching his hand back. "We aren't going anywhere near that!"

"Or that," I said, pointing at a spiky-haired, spiky-toothed monster at the top of the map.

"THE BIG TERROR," read Will.

On the map the monster began jumping up and down and shaking its fists. In the real world, we heard a distant roar.

"So, I guess we are going through the REALLY DARK FOREST?" I said. "I wouldn't mind a torch or something." A torch immediately appeared in my hand.

"That won't work," said Will. "The moment we leave the trap anything we wished up will disappear. Including this map, so we'd better remember it."

Lucky for us there wasn't much to memorize. Our route led through the forest to the SKULL-FACE ROCK. From there we would be able to see the **PIRATE** HIDEOUT. Then all we had to do was get in, get Mum and Dad and get out without being killed.

Of course, you don't have to worry about that. Like I've said quite a few times: nobody dies in this book. It's worth remembering that, because things get pretty perilous from here until the end.

ESCAPE
(NOT FOR THE
FIRST TIME)

Will and I walked through the palm trees towards the forest. Almost immediately, strange things started to happen. With each step, cool stuff popped into existence: huge packets of Lego, dolls, costumes, video games, buckets of sweets, mounds of chocolate, a huge pile of cucumber (I really like cucumber)…

"What's happening?" I asked, as I stepped around a puppy who was licking my ankles.

"It's the trap. It's trying to convince us to stay," Will said.

We walked on, with difficulty. I stumbled over a mound of marshmallows; Will had to

push his way through a huge wall of candy-floss; a whole fun park sprang up behind us.

Then … nothing. It was all gone.

"We're out. Now we just have to get through that," said Will, pointing at a really dark forest.

INTO THE REALLY DARK FOREST

There are all sorts of tactics for dealing with a really dark forest. Here are five of them:

Things Worth Knowing No. 9

by Emilie

1) Don't go in.

2) If you have to go in, stay on the path.

3) If you don't have a path, hire a guide who knows the way.

4) If you don't have a guide, take a map and a compass.

5) If you don't have a path, a guide or a map and a compass, then drop crumbs from a cake as you go so you can find your way out again.

All of those are good ideas, except for the last one. If you have a cake, you are better off just eating it and then following rule No. 1.

Unfortunately, Will and I didn't have any of those options. So we did the only thing we could: we held hands (Will didn't want to but I insisted) and walked into the REALLY DARK FOREST in the hope of going as straight as we could and coming out as quickly as possible.

The problem with our plan was the trees.

They were crammed on top of each other like kids trying to get out of class.

To make matters worse, it really *was* dark. By the time our eyes had adjusted to see where we were going, we had no idea where we had been.

"We're lost," said Will.

"Already?" I asked.

Will turned and pointed to a particularly twisted-looking trunk. "See how the bark makes a horrible face? I've seen that same face three times now."

I looked around. "All the trees are making that face," I said. "Oh no! We're lost!"

I sat down with a bump against one of the horrible trees.

That's when the screaming began.

LOST AND HUNTED

For once, it wasn't me screaming. It wasn't Will either. My first thought was that it must be the trees. It would've made sense given the way they looked. I nearly apologized to the tree behind me; I thought maybe I'd sat on its toes. But it wasn't the trees either.

I wish it had been them. Screaming trees would've been scary, but not nearly as scary as being screamed at by monsters you can't see.

Then the screaming stopped.

"What *was* that?" said Will, who, I noticed, was holding my hand again.

"I don't know," I said. "But it sounded like it had sharp teeth and probably claws. Let's go back."

"OK," Will said. "Which way is back?"

LOST AND HUNTED
(WITH ADDED SCREAMING)

Will and I looked at each other blankly. We were really lost.

REALLY, really, REALLY, really, Really, really, really, really, really, REALLY, REALLY, really, REALLY, REALLY, really, REALLY, really, really lost.

And the thing about being really lost is that you don't know which way anything is: not forwards, not sideways and not back.

We were pondering that problem when a new scream rang out, making us both jump.

"I think we'll call 'back' the opposite direction to that," said Will.

It was a nice idea, but it was rather spoiled by what happened next.

You see, at first the scream came from just one direction. Kind of that way:

But then there was another scream. The monsters were closing in from both directions. Kind of like this:

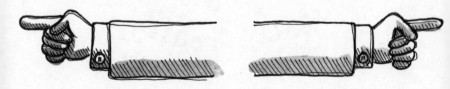

And then there was a third and fourth scream:

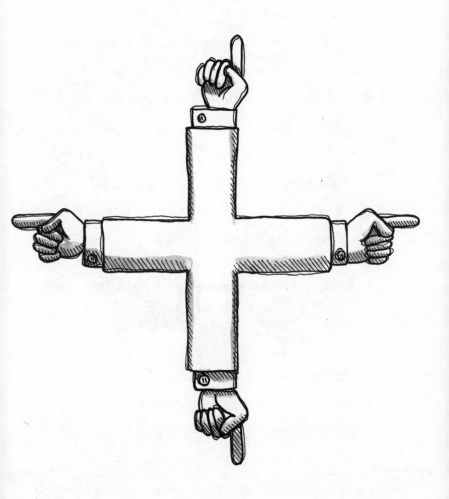

And then...

Horrible "WAAAAAAARKS!", murderous
"KWAAAAAAARKS!" and the odd spine-
chilling "ROOOOAAARK!" were coming from
everywhere. I clapped my hands over my ears.

"We have to go!" shouted Will.

"But which way?"

"It doesn't matter any more," he said. Something dark and massive moved high up in the branches. "We can't stay here!"

So we ran.

WHAT'S BIG, RED AND GOES WAAAAARK!?

We ran past trees, jumped over roots and ducked under branches. Though mostly we ran into trees, tripped over roots and crashed through branches. The forest was so thick I had to put my hands over my face to protect my eyes. That's why I didn't notice when, all of a sudden, the trees stopped. I was so surprised I fell over one last time. Fortunately I landed on something soft.

"Ummphh," said Will. "Get off me."

I lowered my hands from my face and saw a clearing, perhaps ten metres across and nearly perfectly round. On all sides the trees were as thick

as walls. Across the clearing was a
tangle of bamboo. And sitting right
in the centre of the bamboo was the
biggest parrot I had ever seen.

"There's a big parrot over
there," I said to Will.

"I know," replied Will.

"Did you see that it's wearing a little hat?"

"I did see that it's wearing a little hat."

"Did you see that its hat is a **PIRATE**'s
hat?" I asked.

"I did, I did see that it is a **PIRATE**'s hat."

"Did you see that it's looking at us?"

"Yes, I saw that too," said Will. "I am looking at
it looking at us."

Tongue-Twister by Emilie

Do you want to try a tongue-twister?
Say this really fast three times:

A pair of people peered at a PIRATE
parrot, peering at the pair of people
from its parrot perch.

Will stood up and walked, very slowly, towards the parrot.

"Who's a pretty boy?" Will murmured as he edged forward. The bird shuffled on its branch, tilting its head in a way that made it look very much like it was thinking.

"D'you think it understands you?" I asked.

"I doubt it," said Will as he took another step forward.

The bird's head rocked to the other side.

"Polly want a cracker?" Will asked, holding out his empty hand.

The parrot ruffled its feathers. "My name isn't Polly," it said. "And you shouldn't offer crackers if you don't have any."

Then, spreading its wings and rising up to its full height, it let out a deafening

"WAAAAARRRRRK!"

"WAAAAARRRRRK,"

went the trees all around us, and from every side parrots – enormous parrots – flew into the clearing.

They were red, green, yellow and orange and sometimes all of those colours at once. Most wore some bit of **PIRATE** clothing and *all* of them were screeching.

It was the noise we'd heard in the forest, which came as something of a relief. I'd kind of assumed something like this was chasing us:

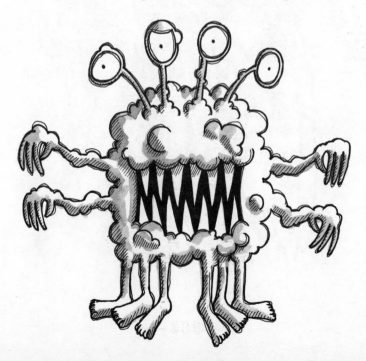

Which is clearly worse than this:

THE MEETING

The parrots filled the branches around the clearing, all the time squawking so loudly I wanted to pull my ears off and tuck them in my pockets.

"Fellow parrots! Fellow parrots!" Pirate-Hat shouted above the squawking. "QUIET!"

The birds hushed down until the only noise was them shuffling on their perches and the occasional crack of a nut. Many of them seemed to have brought peanuts.

Pirate-Hat drew itself up to its full height and cleared its throat. "Item one on the meeting agenda," it said. "What should be done about the **PIRATES**?"

The parrots started squawking all over again.

Pirate-Hat waved its wing sternly. "One at a time!" it shouted.

"Drop them in the SAND BOG OF CERTAIN DOOM!" yelled one parrot.

"Feed them to THE BIG TERROR!" screeched another.

"Tickle their toes with belly feathers!" shouted a small bird with a giggle.

Will and I looked at each other. Until that moment we'd assumed the parrots were on the **PIRATES'** side. Instead, we seemed to have stumbled across allies. I was quite relieved ... for a moment.

"Motions have been tabled," said Pirate-Hat. "Let's vote. Those in favour of dropping these two **PIRATES** in the SAND BOG, squawk now!"

Will and I both jumped to our feet.

"Hang on," said Will.

Pirate-Hat turned slowly to look at my brother. "**PIRATES** are not permitted to speak at

parrot meetings," it said.

"But we are not—" I began. Pirate-Hat cut me off with a swoosh of its wing and a "Shush!"

"You have made a mista—"

"I SAID SHUSH!" the parrot screeched. Then turning back to the other birds, it said, "Those parrots in favour of feeding the **PIRATES** to THE BIG TERROR, squawk now."

There was a horrendous racket as the birds all screeched as one.

"The WAAARKS have it!" boomed Pirate-Hat. "THE BIG TERROR will feast on **PIRATE** tonight!"

WHY I HATE
STARFISH

Here's something you don't know about me.

I hate starfish.

I bet you don't know anyone who hates starfish. Well, now you do.

I hate them heaps!

It started with a show-and-tell at school. We had to bring in something from the sea and I brought in an old starfish I found on the beach.

I'd worked really hard on a presentation (OK, I Googled starfish, but it was still good stuff). I was going to say how starfish are not fish, how they were around before the dinosaurs and how they are carnivores. I was going to say all that, but when I stood in front of the class I got so

Show
and
Tell

nervous I couldn't breathe. Because I couldn't breathe, I couldn't speak. And because I couldn't speak, I just stood there.

The teacher kept asking me to start, but I couldn't speak, not even to tell her I couldn't speak.

Then the kids began to giggle.

Eventually I managed just one word – "Starfish" – and I held the starfish on top of my head. I must've looked like an ocean-themed Christmas tree.

The class exploded with laughter.

For weeks afterwards, children ran up to me in the playground, shoved their hands in the air and shouted "Starfish!" before falling about laughing.

That was the last time I tried to make a speech. Until now.

HOW I BECAME A PIRATE

I got to my feet.

"This is unfair!" I shouted at the parrots. "You chase us through this REALLY DARK FOREST, scare us to bits, make me feel daft by turning out not to be a four-eyed, six-legged monster, and now, *now* you're going to feed us—"

Pirate-Hat cut me off with a thunderous squawk.

"IT IS NOT YOUR TURN TO SPEAK!" it shouted.

I'd had enough of being screeched at.

"When *can* I speak, you oversized budgerigar?!" I shouted back.

Pirate-Hat turned to me. "You may speak now."

Turning to the rest of the birds, I said, "Good parrots of this awful forest. We are not **PIRATES**."

The parrots all began squawking.

"Of course you are," cried Pirate-Hat. "**PIRATES** are people, aren't they?"

"I guess so," I said.

"And you are people. So you must be **PIRATES**!" The assembled birds cheered their approval.

This was ridiculous. I was beginning to understand why stupid people are called "bird-brained".

"OK!" I shouted. "Well, chickens are birds, aren't they?"

"Yes," said Pirate-Hat.

"And you are all birds, aren't you?"

"Of course."

"Then you must be chickens. And this is a *parrot* meeting, so none of you should be here."

"She has a point," said a parrot with an eye-patch. "If we're all chickens then we're at the wrong meeting."

"We are not chickens!" squawked Pirate-Hat.

"Well, if you can be a bird but not a chicken, then we can be people but not **PIRATES**," I said.

"OK," said Pirate-Hat. "What are you then?"

HOW I BECAME A PARROT

I thought for a second.

"How about this," I said. "You all hate **PIRATES**, don't you?"

"We do!" the parrots cried.

"We used to work for them," said Pirate-Hat. "We had to sit on their rancid shoulders and shout silly things like 'Pieces of eight' and 'Walk the plank'. It was humiliating."

Another parrot took up the story. "Ten hours a day, plus overtime up the mast. And we were paid peanuts."

"I quite liked the peanuts," said another parrot, to general approval from the birds.

"Anyway," I said, "it's clear that parrots hate

PIRATES."

The birds squawked their agreement.

"Well, *we* hate **PIRATES** too!" I declared. "In fact, we're heading to their hideout now to fight them." To judge by the number of heads tilting to one side or the other, the parrots weren't following. "Sooo …" I said, "if parrots hate **PIRATES**, and we hate **PIRATES**, then *we* must be parrots!"

COMRADES IN WINGS

My argument was shaky, not least because I had just established that all parrots are chickens.

"You don't LOOK like parrots," said a green and orange bird.

It had a point.

"Sure, we don't have feathers or beaks," I said. "But is that what really makes a parrot a parrot?"

"Yes," said one of the parrots.

"No!" I said. "It isn't how you look that makes you a parrot. It's what's in here." I thumped my chest where I thought my heart was. "A parrot is a parrot because of how it acts, how it feels – and because it hates **PIRATES**."

I was shouting now.
"Comrades, we are ALL
parrots!"

There was a huge
cheer.

"And parrots
don't feed parrots to
monsters!" I punched
the air triumphantly.

The cheering stopped.
A couple of the birds
whistled nervously.

"Well, the thing is,"
said Pirate-Hat, "we voted to feed you to the
monster."

"So?" I said.

"Rules are rules and a vote is a vote," it said.
"If we went around ignoring votes we'd be no
better than the PIRATES."

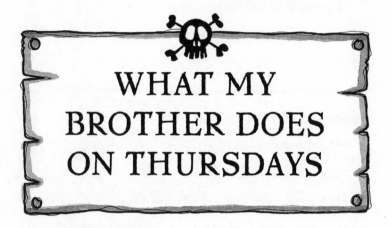

WHAT MY BROTHER DOES ON THURSDAYS

Things weren't quite working out how I'd hoped.

Then Will put his hand up.

"Excuse me," he said. "What would happen if not all the parrots at the meeting had voted?"

"Impossible," said Pirate-Hat. "It's against the rules."

"That's what I thought," said Will. "Specifically, it would breach Article Two of the Parrots' Universal Suffrage Act of 1821."

I had no idea what he was on about. Neither did the birds, to judge by the number of parrots with their heads tipping side-to-side.

"I guess so," Pirate-Hat said, a little unsurely.

"Good," said Will. "Well, I was at the meeting and I didn't vote. And we just agreed that I am a parrot. That confused-looking parrot in her nightie didn't vote either." He pointed at me.

"Yes, but—" said Pirate-Hat.

"*Quod erat demonstrandum*, the vote was illegal."

"Quod erat what?" said Pirate-Hat.

"QED!" exclaimed Will.

"QED?" I asked.

"Yes indeed," said Will.

RISKYPEDIA
The Adventurer's Encyclopedia

>> QUOD ERAT DEMONSTRANDUM (QED)
Quod erat demonstrandum, usually referred to by its initials QED, is a Latin phrase that basically means, "See! I told you so." Smart people say QED at the end of an argument to make themselves feel smarter. Really smart people tend to avoid people who say QED.

A particularly old parrot with a wooden leg, a monocle and a pipe raised its wing. "The big parrot without feathers has a point," it said.

"Does he?" said Pirate-Hat. "I don't understand anything he says."

"If they are off to fight the **PIRATES**, it seems a pity to stop them," said another parrot.

"True," said Pirate-Hat. "I suppose we could vote to *ignore* the old vote."

The parrots squawked their approval.

I shuffled closer to Will.

"All that stuff you said?"

"Oh that," said Will.

"Where did you learn that?" I asked.

"Well, the thing is," said Will, looking down at his feet. "I kind of, that is to say, ummm, you

know how on Thursdays I go to a friend's house
after school?"

"Yeah."

"Well, I do go to a house," he said. "Only it's
a courthouse."

I looked at Will in dismay, wondering if
anything he'd said in the past year was true.

"I work as a lawyer. But don't tell Mum or
Dad, they'd be really disappointed."

"About the lying?"

Will shook his head. "About me having such
an awful job."

NOTHING CHANGES

The parrot meeting dragged on.

More votes were called. There was one to make meetings more inclusive of people who are actually parrots. Another was called to consider changing the name of the REALLY DARK FOREST to something more likely to encourage tourism. There was a motion to count how many chickens were present at the meeting. Will and I sat down to wait.

EVERYTHING CHANGES

Our situation was still hopeless. We were still lost in the forest, we still had no parents and the **PIRATES** were still winning. Only it was worse now, because we were also stuck in a meeting that was never, ever, *ever* going to end. I got up on my knees and yawned, stretching my arms high above my head.

"Yes?" said Pirate-Hat.

"What?" I said.

"You put your arm ... er, wing up. Do you want to vote on something?"

"OK," I said. "Let's vote on how you can help us get out of this forest."

I was expecting squawking. Instead there was

silence, broken only by the crack of a peanut shell.

"Aren't we going to vote?" I asked.

"Why would we?" said Pirate-Hat.

"Oh come *on*!" I yelled, waking up Will, who had fallen asleep next to me. "You've voted on everything else, why not this?"

The parrots looked at each other.

"No point in voting on that," said Pirate-Hat. "All you have to do is go out through the exit."

"What are you on about?" I said. "We've run over every inch of this forest, most of them twice, and haven't seen any way out."

Pirate-Hat shrugged. "You didn't look over there," it said, pointing across the clearing to a door marked EXIT.

Will and I looked at the door, and then

at each other. Then we looked at the door again.

"Well," said Will. "We'd best get going."

And that's what we did. We picked ourselves up off the ground and walked through the door.

A door that led straight to the **PIRATES**.

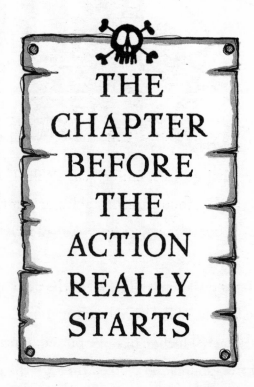

THE CHAPTER BEFORE THE ACTION REALLY STARTS

Actually, it wasn't straight to the **PIRATES**.

The exit opened onto a wide field of grass bathed in the light of the setting sun.

To our left was a boulder, on which the evening shadows had marked out depressions that looked like eye sockets.

"SKULL-FACE ROCK," I said.

"Say what you see, Emilie," said Will. Then, pointing to a group of picnic tables on our right, he said, "I suppose you're going to tell me that's the PICNIC AREA?"

I punched Will on the shoulder, but not hard.

"A picnic would be nice," I said.

"Yeah," my brother agreed. "But I'm not sure I like the view."

In the distance an imposing castle loomed menacingly (scary castles always loom) and from the castle's highest tower a **PIRATE** flag flapped in the wind.

"The **PIRATE** HIDEOUT," I said needlessly.

"Yep," said Will. "The **PIRATE** HIDEOUT."

LOOMING

By the time we reached the **PIRATE** HIDEOUT, night had fallen. The castle, which had loomed scarily from a distance, loomed terrifyingly up close. About the only thing that could have made the castle look any scarier was a lightning storm. Then, because this is one of "those" stories, thunder rumbled in the dark and lightning split the sky.

It began to rain.

OUR PLAN

I turned to Will.

"So what's our plan?" I asked.

Will looked up at the castle.

I stayed very quiet. I didn't want to disturb him while he came up with our plan. We'd need a plan, of course, a really cunning one. The **PIRATES** were murderous and numerous. We were two kids in wet nightwear.

We needed the sort of plan only Will could come up with.

I looked up at my brother, full of admiration.

"I thought," he said, "we would walk up those stairs and go in through the front door."

I looked at Will some more, mostly in the hope that he had something else to say. The

longer he stayed silent, the more my hope
ebbed. In its place flowed disbelief.

"Is that our whole plan?"

"It's all I could think of just now."

"It sucks!"

Will looked a little hurt.

"There's no other way in," he said, as he
began walking to the bottom of a huge
staircase.

"This is the worst plan ever!"
I shouted as I followed him.

"What did you want?"
he asked.

"Something better than this! This is not the sort of plan someone should have to get into a **PIRATE** HIDEOUT. It's the sort of plan I would come up with to get into a friend's house."

Will shrugged.

"You know what," I continued, "it's not even a plan. It's just a thing we're doing right before we get caught."

As I complained, we walked up the steps. In fact, I was so busy complaining I didn't notice us climbing. Before I knew it we were standing before an oversized wooden door.

When I saw the door, I stopped complaining.

It was just a wooden door, one that could do with a bit of paint. But it was terrifying.

"Well," said Will. "This is it."

MY BRAVERY

I looked at the door. The **PIRATES** were behind it. *McSnottbeard* was behind it. The only chance of getting our family back was behind it.

My knees gave out. Will grabbed me. "You don't have to go in," he said. "I can probably handle it by myself."

I am not very brave – as I've already said. And at that moment, as I lay in Will's

arms, I was absolutely petrified. I simply couldn't bring myself to go through that door. What was the point? Two kids had, at best, a one in one million chance against a gang of **PIRATES**.

But one kid all alone had even less chance.

I stood back up. Almost every part of me wanted to run away – and the bits that didn't wanted to cry – but I balled my hand into a fist, reached out and knocked on the door.

I looked at Will. I expected to see relief and gratitude – perhaps even love – as he realized I wasn't going to abandon him. What I saw was confusion.

"What are you doing?" he said.

"I'm going in with you. I can't let you face the **PIRATES** all alone."

"That's nice. BUT I WASN'T GOING TO KNOCK!"

"Oh," I said.

And then the door opened. And my knees gave way again.

"Hello," said my mother.

MUM!

"Mum?" I said.

"Mum?" said Will.

"MUM!" we shouted together.

I ran through the doorway and jumped into her arms, then bounced off her and hit the ground with a bump. She hadn't caught me!

I rubbed my backside as I stood up. "Mum, are you OK?"

She didn't move.

"That's not Mum," said Will.

"Huh?"

"It's a copy."

"How d'you know?" I asked.

"She didn't catch you," he said. "Real mums catch a kid who jumps into their arms."

Fake-Mum turned away, and in a cheerful voice said, "Follow me, please."

I stood there open-mouthed as she walked off.

"What do we do?" I eventually asked Will.

"Follow her," said Will.

"Really?"

"Sure."

We walked after Fake-Mum.

I was still confused, and things got a lot more confusing a second later. Out of a door just ahead of us Mum appeared again. She was carrying a feather duster. This was seriously weird, mainly because we could still see the first Mum, walking away down the corridor.

"Mum?" I said to Number 2.

She stopped briefly, but only to dust a picture frame, before she walked through a second door.

"Another copy," said Will.

I looked through the door where Mum Number 2 had gone. There was another Mum cleaning away vegetable peelings in the kitchen, and another washing out a pot.

"Will!" I said. "There are *heaps* of Mums."

"Let's just keep our eyes on that one." Will pointed at Fake-Mum Number 1. "She seems to know where she's going."

Number 1 led us into a room with two sofas, a fireplace and a TV in the corner. It was just like our living room at home. And even more so because lying on the sofa watching the TV was our dad.

"Dad!" I shouted. I would've run to him, but Will held me back.

"It's another copy," Will said.

"How do you—?"

"He's lying on a sofa."

"So what?"

"He isn't asleep."

"Good point," I said. "Definitely a copy."

Fake-Mum Number 1 had stopped in front of a door that led out the other side of the room. She turned to us and in a hollow, cheerful voice said, "Wait here. I will tell the **PIRATES** they have visitors."

And she walked out.

WAITING

Will sat down on the sofa from which Fake-Dad
was staring at the TV.

"What are you doing?" I asked.

"Waiting."

"For what?"

"The **PIRATES**."

"OK," I said. "I thought we would sneak
around trying to find Mum and Dad without,
you know, actually *meeting* the **PIRATES**."

"You should've thought of that before you
knocked on the front door."

He had a point. I pushed Fake-Dad's feet off
the sofa and sat down next to Will.

"What are we going to do when they get
here?" I asked.

"Ask them to give Mum and Dad back."

"I don't think that's going to work."

Will shrugged. "Neither do I."

FEAR OF THE UNKNOWN

I have a theory about what happened next. It goes something like this:

When the **PIRATES** walked into the room, what they saw was two kids sitting on a sofa waiting for them. The same two kids who had just knocked on their front door. If you are a **PIRATE**, this isn't what you expect from kids. What you expect is a lot of screaming, a fair bit of running away and, as a last resort, some cowering.

We weren't doing any of that. As far as the **PIRATES** were concerned, that clearly meant we knew something they didn't. And whatever that thing was, it meant we weren't afraid. And as anyone who is about to get in a fight knows, when the other person isn't afraid, then *you* probably should be.

That's why the **PIRATES** didn't kill us straight away. They were looking for a trap, and until they could work out what it was, they were being careful.

"Arrrrr," said *McSnottbeard*, because, as I've already said, **PIRATES** start every sentence that way. "Ye shouldn't have come here. I am going to kill ye." He drew his cutlass and pointed it at us.

PIRATES aren't much for small talk.

"No you aren't," said Will, calmly lying back on the sofa.

McSnottbeard lowered his sword. "I'm not?" he asked.

"Nope," said Will. "You're going to give us back our parents."

"I surely arrren't," *McSnottbeard* said, taking a hesitant step forward. "I am going to keep them. And I am going to kill you."

Will swivelled to face the **PIRATE**. I got ready to run, scream and cower.

"No," said Will, putting a hand on my knee to keep me where I was. "You're going to do exactly what I want. And the first thing I want is for you to answer a question."

"Why would I do tharrrrt?"

"It would make things easier on you in the long run."

McSnottbeard burst out laughing in a way that suggested he wasn't at all worried about the long run. But he didn't move any closer.

"OK," *McSnottbeard* said. "What do you periwinkles want to know?"

"Why'd you take our parents?" asked Will.

"Because we needed 'em," said *McSnottbeard*,

taking another step towards us, albeit a small one. "Now, I am going to kill you."

"Before you do," said Will, "*why* do you need our parents?"

McSnottbeard waved his cutlass at us. "Same reason anyone needs parents. To clean up, make sure we take a barrrrrth now and then, and to cook our dinner. Now, I am going to kill you."

"Before you do," said Will, "why did you clone them?"

McSnottbeard groaned and lowered his cutlass. "Because the real ones were horrible. Your mum was always shushing us and your dad tried to make us eat beans. Said it would be good for us."

The **PIRATES** all shuddered.

"The clones arrrrre better," said *McSnottbeard*. "They just do the things we want."

"Except for the Dad clones," said a girl **PIRATE** holding a large musket. "All they do is lie around."

"Well, why not give us the originals?" I said. "We take them home, you keep the clones, everyone is happy and nobody has to die."

It was a good solution. Any reasonable person would have agreed to that.

Unfortunately, **PIRATES** aren't reasonable.

PIRATES AREN'T
REASONABLE

McSnottbeard shook his head. "Can't do that."

"Why not?" I asked.

"Too nice. People'd hear about it and my reputation would be ruined. Without a reputation for nastiness a **PIRATE** is just a sailor with poor personal hygiene. Anyway, your parents look good in the zoo."

"You really put them in a zoo?" I asked.

"Course we did. And don't think you can get 'em out," growled the **PIRATE** king. "Thaaar cage is locked and I have the

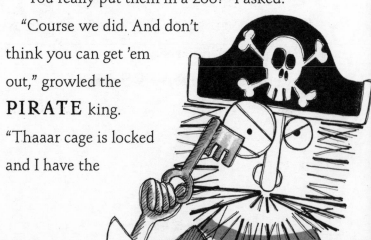

only key." He pulled a huge iron key out of his pocket. "And now, no more questions – 'tis time to die!"

McSnottbeard strode towards us.

"STOP!" shouted Will, standing up and spreading his arms. "Know this! I am William the **PIRATE** hunter, scourge of buccaneers, feared by bandits of all the seven seas and quite a few lakes. And you are under arrest for parent stealing. Put down your cutlasses, knives, guns and, um, bit of wood with nails in it. Give yourselves up!"

"Give up?" asked *McSnottbeard*.

"Surrender!" growled Will.

"Why?" said *McSnottbeard*.

"Because if you don't, we'll make you!"

I got up off the sofa and stood next to Will. It didn't make us any scarier, but it was the right thing to do.

The **PIRATES** drew their swords, hefted their bits of wood and aimed their guns.

McSnottbeard raised his cutlass above his head and took a stride towards us.

"You." Stride.

"Will." Stride.

"Make US?!"

The **PIRATE**

king was

standing

right

over us

now. His

face was

twisted

with rage.

His eyes

had turned red

and spittle dripped

down his beard.

"You and what army?" he snarled.

Will, who was nose-to-nose with *McSnottbeard*, smiled and took a step back. He mumbled some words that ended with "abracadabra" and clapped his hands together. "THIS ARMY!" he shouted.

The air rippled. There was a kind of sucking noise, followed by a pop from behind us. And then silence. I turned around to see what had made the noise.

I stared. You would've stared too. Anyone would've.

OUR ARMY

I turned back to Will, who was still looking at *McSnottbeard* and the **PIRATES**. They weren't looking at Will or me any more.

"Will," I said, "there are three dinosaurs behind us."

"Yes," he said.

"And some zombies."

"Yes."

"There are lots of parrots."

"I expect so."

"Count Salazar is there. And Yeth."

"Thuprise," said Yeth, waving a mop in the **PIRATES'** direction.

"Will," I said, "there is a werewolf there.

There *aren't* even any werewolves in this story. They were pretend."

"Not any more," said Will.

"Your stuffed monkey doll is there, and it's wearing a dress."

My brother looked around for the first time. "That's a mistake."

SURRENDER

He turned back to the **PIRATES**.

"Put down your weapons," Will growled.

Swords, pistols, daggers, a musket and a plank of wood clattered to the floor. All the **PIRATES** put their hands up.

All the **PIRATES** except *McSnottbeard*. He was still holding his cutlass above our heads.

"*McSnottbeard*," said Will, "it's over. Give us the key."

McSnottbeard looked at the army behind us. He looked back at his **PIRATES**. He looked at us.

"Aaaay, you arrre right, it's over," he said with a nod. "But it ain't finished."

The handle of *McSnottbeard*'s cutlass came

down hard on Will's head. There was a horrible crack and Will crumpled to the ground.

McSnottbeard turned and ran.

I stood open-mouthed.

HOW TO WIN
AND STILL LOSE

I watched the **PIRATE** disappear through a door. It took a second to work out what had happened. *McSnottbeard* was gone. We'd won. My heart flopped with relief. Hearts usually leap with relief, but I'd been through so much that my heart was exhausted.

"We won," I said to no one in particular.

I looked down at Will, who was lying on the floor. He looked like he was sleeping. I dropped to my knees and took his head in my hands.

"Will," I said, "we won."

Nothing.

"William?" I always call him William when

I'm being serious, and all of a sudden I was seriously worried.

His body was limp. Blood flowed from beneath his hair. I leaned down and put my ear to his nose. There was no noise. No breath.

Will was dead.

DEAD

Oh yeah. That thing I said, right at the start of this book, about no one dying? That wasn't completely true.

What I should've said was: nobody dies in this book – except my brother.

DEAD-ISH

Actually, what I should've said is: nobody *is* dead by the end of this book.

NOTHING
THERIOUTH

"Perhaps I can be of thome help," said a voice
from behind me.

I turned around to see Yeth shuffling forward.

"I think your brother may have patht away,"
he said.

I still couldn't understand him.

"He's not breathing," I said.

Yeth nodded.

"He's dead."

Yeth nodded again.

I burst into tears.

"Oh dear," said Yeth.

"William is dead!" I wailed.

"Yeth," said Yeth.

"Thankfully it'th nothing theriouth."

I was still holding on to Will's head as Yeth bent down over my brother.

"A little death never hurt anyone," he said, running his hands over Will's limp body. "No, quite the oppothite. Good for the health to die every now and then. Remindth a perthon to look after themthelveth. That'th what my mum thays. She hath died five times herthelf and is thtill very much alive."

Yeth placed his hands over Will's chest. "Thith tends to thting a bit."

A shock of energy zapped through Will. His body jolted then went limp.

"Give it a thecond," said Yeth.

And then Will's eyes snapped open.

ALIVE

"You're alive!" I shouted.

Will let out a whimper, then breathed in deeply. His eyes turned to mine.

"*McSnottbeard*?" he said.

"No, it's Emilie. Your sister."

"I know," Will groaned. "Where *is* *McSnottbeard*?"

"Oh," I said. "It's OK. He's gone."

Will shook his head. "It's not OK. He has the key to our parents' cage."

Will rolled onto his side and pushed himself up on one elbow, before carefully rising to his feet.

"We have to catch him," Will said, as his eyes rolled into the back of his head and he fell to the ground.

"Will?" I said.

His eyes snapped open. *"McSnottbeard."*

"Nope, still me," I said.

"Which way did he go?"

"Through that door."

"Let's get him." Will stood, took an unsteady step in the wrong direction and fell over again. It turns out that being dead really takes it out of you.

Will lay there for a good while, breathing but unconscious.

As he lay there, I noticed something really

weird. It wasn't the presence of three dinosaurs, an evil warlock, a handful of zombies and a monkey in a dress. It wasn't even the gang of defeated **PIRATES** who were trying to look as unthreatening as possible. No, the weird thing was that, with my brother asleep, everyone was looking at *me* to tell them what to do next.

I reacted in the only reasonable way I could: I began slapping Will's face to wake him up.

It took quite a few slaps.

THE HERO

"*McSnottbeard*?" said Will, when his eyes
finally opened again.

"Still me."

"You're going to have to go after him."

That was more like it. Things felt better with
my brother in charge.

"Yep. Let's go," I said.

"Not *we*. You."

I stared at Will.

"I can't walk Emilie," he said. "My head is
spinning."

"Thath a thide effect of being recently dead,"
said Yeth.

"We can wait," I said.

Will shook his head. "*McSnottbeard* is getting

away."

I stared some more.

"It's up to you," said Will.

I stared.

"You have to catch *McSnottbeard*."

I stared.

"You have to get the key."

I stared.

"Emilie, please stop staring at me," said Will.

"Me? Just me?" My voice sounded tiny. "Against *McSnottbeard*?"

Will nodded.

"But you're meant to do this part," I said. "You are the brave one. You are the hero of this story."

"No," said Will softly.

"Yes," I said. "It's written on page nine of this book."

"It says 'Nobody dies' on the cover," said Will. "You can't believe everything you read."

"But," I said.

"It's you Emilie," said Will. "It's always been you."

I shook my head. "But I'm always scared."

Now it was Will's turn to shake his head. "Doesn't matter," he said. "Being scared isn't the opposite of being brave, it's just the measure of how brave you can be."

Will took my hand in his. "You never give up Emilie. You were scared when our parents were stolen but you climbed out of the sinking house. You thought we would be roasted when we jumped into the volcano, but you jumped. You told off a warlock. You made the parrots listen. You even stood up to fight the **PIRATES**."

"I *did* do all that," I said, feeling a little impressed with myself.

"Brave isn't how you feel, Emilie. It's what you do. You are the bravest person I know. You are the hero of this story."

"I am?"

"You are to me."

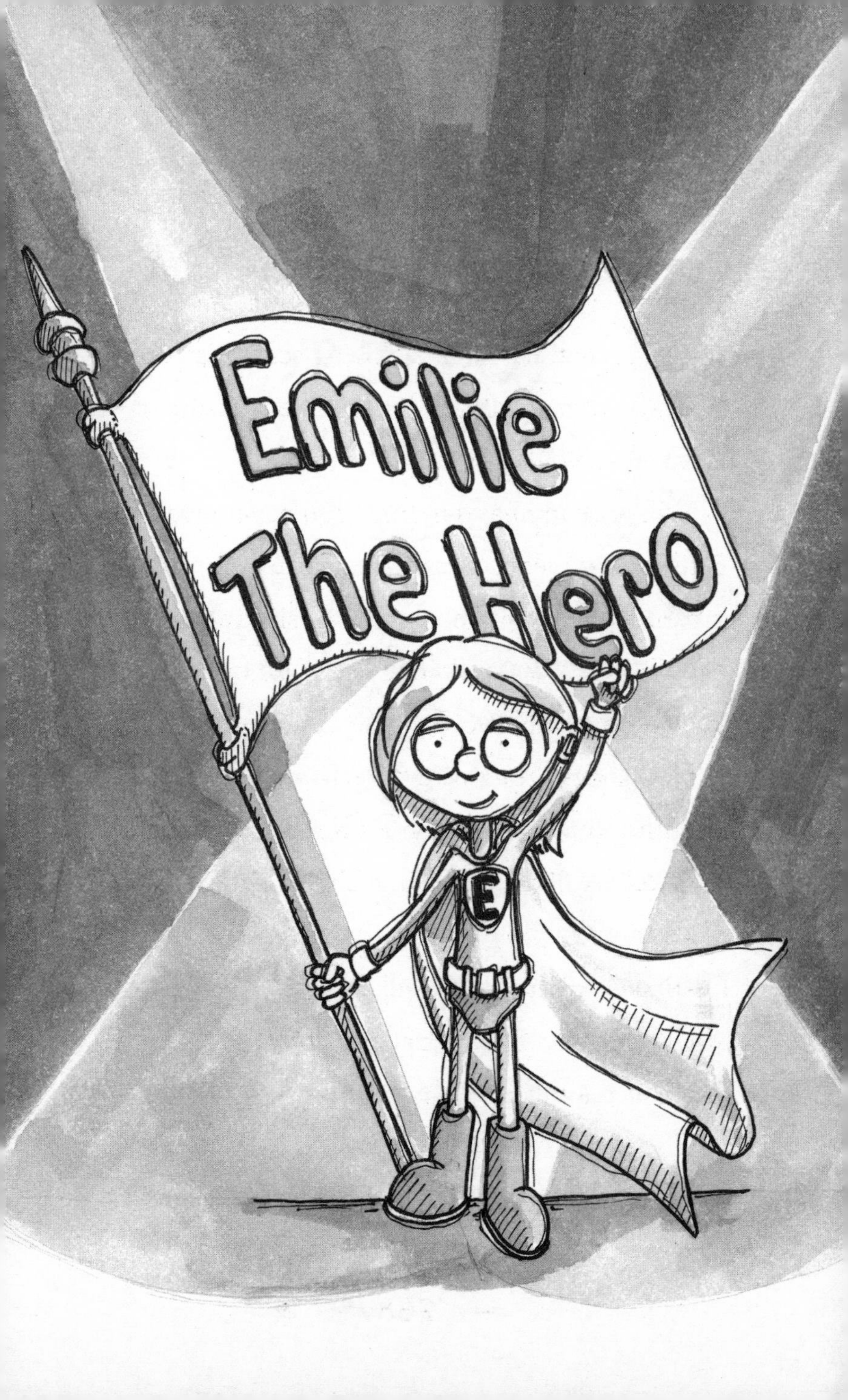
Emilie
The Hero

IT'S OK
TO LIE TO
PIRATES

The problem with people saying nice things about you is that it makes you want to be the person they say you are. After Will's speech, I *had* to go after *McSnottbeard*, even if I was hoping I wouldn't find him.

No such luck.

I could smell him through every twist and turn of the hideout and all the way to the top of a steep spiral staircase.

"More stairs," I groaned, and began to climb.

The higher I climbed, the stronger the smell of **PIRATE** became, and the stronger the smell, the closer I was to *McSnottbeard*. Quite soon I could hear him as well as smell him. He appeared to be making up a song.

> *"Nooooo, they'll never catch me,*
> *Nooooo, they'll never get the key.*
> *Gonna throw it deep in the bottom of the sea,*
> *Nooooo … something … something … pee."*

I gasped. If he threw the key away my parents would be stuck in a cage for ever.

I gasped too loudly.

"Who's there?" shouted *McSnottbeard*.

"Ummm," I said. "Emilie."

"Just you?" the **PIRATE** growled and started down the steps towards me.

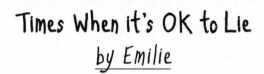

Times When it's OK to Lie
by Emilie

1) When your parents ask if you are tired.

2) When anyone asks if you still have space for ice cream.

3) When a PIRATE asks if you are alone.

"I wouldn't come any closer," I shouted up the stairs. "The werewolf is here and he's angry."

"I can't hear him."

"Woof," I said.

"That doesn't sound angry," said *McSnottbeard*. "Doesn't sound like a werewolf either."

The sound of **PIRATE** boots clomping down the stairs got closer.

I screamed.

"What was that?" asked *McSnottbeard*.

It took me a second to realize he was talking about my scream.

"It's the parrots," I lied. "There's loads of them."

Now it was *McSnottbeard*'s turn to scream.

"PARROTS?!" he shouted and ran back up the stairs. "You'll never catch me!"

I ran after him, barking and screaming every so often to make sure he didn't turn around.

BAD

By the time I reached the top of the stairs, I had stopped barking and screaming in favour of just puffing.

Next to the last stair was a wooden door, which I leant against to catch my breath. Then I took a step back and ran at it.

My shoulder crunched into the door, smashing it open, just like in the movies – before my momentum carried me forwards and I fell off the tower's ledge, which is the way things tend to go in real life.

As I plunged into empty space I shot out a hand to grab hold of something and was amazed to find I'd succeeded. And there I swung by a single hand, grasping a thin iron

railing that ran around the narrow ledge of
the highest tower of a **PIRATE** HIDEOUT
perched on the side of a cliff that plunged into
an angry sea.

Oh, and it was raining. And windy too. And
there was lightning, plenty of it.

At least things can't get any worse, I thought to
myself.

And then they did.

WORSE

My hand began to slip.

I was holding on with four fingers.

Three.

Two.

One.

None.

I fell.

Or at least I would have, but as
I slipped a huge gust of wind
whooshed up the side of the
tower and I whooshed up with it. I whooshed
so far I went straight past the ledge I'd fallen off
and onto the roof.

I landed with a thud and dug my fingers into
the slippery tiles.

Lightning cracked across the sky.

And in the flash of light, I saw *McSnottbeard* next to me.

PANTS

I probably wouldn't have found the **PIRATE**
if gravity hadn't taken a brief holiday and left
the wind in charge of falling.

And not only had I found him, but I'd found
the key too. It was in *McSnottbeard*'s hand just
above me. All I had to do was reach out and
grab it. The problem was that I was using my
hands, both of them, to hold on to the wet roof.

When I stretched to grab the key I slid.
Instead of the key I ended up with a fistful of
McSnottbeard's trousers.

The **PIRATE**'s head whipped around.

"Gerr off it," he said. "Yaaar pulling me
strides down."

It was true. Each time I tried to climb up

his clothes to the key,
McSnottbeard's tattered
trousers slipped lower and I
slipped with them.

Quite soon I could see
his underpants – they had
hearts on them.

This can't be the last thing I see before I die, I
thought to myself. I let go of his trousers and
dug my fingers back into the tiles.

McSnottbeard smiled evilly down at me,
pulled his bottoms up and scrambled to the top
of the tower.

Lightning cracked through the sky as he
pulled himself upright on the flagpole.

"Ha harrr! Ye have failed," the **PIRATE**
laughed above the roar of the storm. "Nae
wee bilge-burb could ever defeat the great
McSnottbeard! I am supremely wicked! I am
superbly vile! I am—"

"Wearing love-heart underpants!" I yelled as I

clawed my way up the tiles to within inches
of him.

I reached out to grab *McSnottbeard*'s ankle,
but as I did he lifted his foot, then stamped
down on my hand.

Pain shot up my arm as my fingers were
crushed beneath his boot.

I cried out in agony.

The **PIRATE** grinned evilly. "As I was
saying," he snarled, "ye have failed."

Then, still
watching me,
he raised the key
above his head,
pulled his arm back and
prepared to hurl my parents'
freedom into the waves below.

ZAP!

McSnottbeard was looking down, so he didn't see the crackle and glow in the clouds above him. But I did.

Tiny electrical sparks jumped off the key in the **PIRATE**'s hand as he began his throw.

I shouted the only thing I could think of to make him stop: "DOUBLOONS!"

McSnottbeard froze.

"What about 'em?!" he growled down to me.

"In my hand," I said, nodding towards the fingers trapped under his boot.

"Give 'em to me," said the **PIRATE**, lifting his foot.

The cloud flashed as I snatched my hand back. I looked up at *McSnottbeard*.

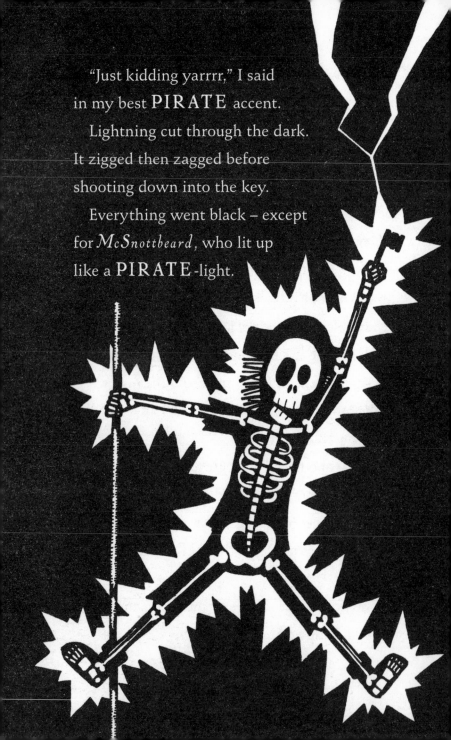

"Just kidding yarrrr," I said
in my best PIRATE accent.

Lightning cut through the dark.
It zigged then zagged before
shooting down into the key.

Everything went black – except
for *McSnottbeard*, who lit up
like a PIRATE-light.

Then, as quickly as the lightning struck, it disappeared.

McSnottbeard froze for a second, two seconds, then slumped to the bottom of the flagpole, before sliding past me, off the edge of the wet roof and into the darkness.

Over the howl of the wind I heard a faint shout of "Arrrrrrrrr" and then a distant splash.

Cripes! I thought as I slid slowly down the roof and dropped carefully onto the ledge.

Next to me *McSnottbeard*'s hat gently smouldered.

"Smoked like a kipper," I said as I bent down to pick it up.

I yelped as I lifted the hat, and only partly because I burnt myself on the embers around its brim.

Beneath the hat was the key.

EPILOGUE

And that was that.

I mean, I could tell you all about walking back down the steps, but nothing happened. Will was sitting up when I reached him and, with a bit of help, he was even able to come with me to get Mum and Dad (one of the **PIRATES** showed us where they were).

The key worked, which was a relief after all I'd been through. There were lots of cuddles and a few tears, mainly from me.

Count Salazar used a bit of hocus pocus to help us get back home (or at least to the place where the house had been, which had thankfully dried out). We took a couple of the clones back with us. The Mum-clones helped us rebuild. The Dad-clones mainly lay on the sofa giving instructions.

And that was that.

Nobody was dead and the hero (ME!) had made sure everyone lived happily ever after.

Happily until the day that alien slug-monsters kidnapped my parents, that is.

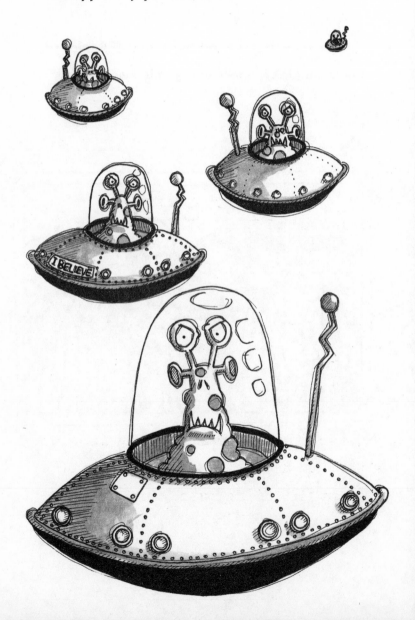

THE END

PS That bit right at the start about how a hero makes sure there are no more scary things after you say "THE END"? You shouldn't believe that either.

ABOUT THE AUTHOR

*Paul Whitfield was born in Australia, and has,
mostly by accident, been a business journalist since
1997. He has written for Bloomberg, the BBC, the
New York Times and several British national newspapers.
Pirate McSnottbeard in the Zombie Terror
Rampage is his first full-length novel for children.
He is currently writing the second book in
the Pirate McSnottbeard series.*